Frieda's Locket

Frieda's Locket
Based on a True Story

Paula Michele Williams

2007

Frieda's Locket

CONTENTS

Dedicated to my grandparents,
Frieda and Bruce Miller

CHAPTER ONE
Goodbye to Germany

1911

Frieda lovingly stroked the gold locket hanging from a gold chain around her neck. Her parents, Abraham and Catharine Brierley, had just given her the locket as a bon voyage gift.

"Oh Papa! Mama! I love it!"

"Open the heart and look inside, Frieda."

"Oh my! Pictures of you and Mama! Thank you. I'll treasure it until the day I die!"

"Whenever you get lonely or homesick in America, all you have to do is open your locket and there we will be!" Papa reassured her.

At twenty, Friederike Marianne Charlotte Brierley, who liked to be called Frieda, was considered by many to be a beauty. She had a shapely, petite figure with a rather large bosom for her five foot stature, and a very slim waist which was accentuated in her corset. Her high cheek bones supported her strikingly beautiful transparent eyes of greenish blue. She wore her golden blond hair braided and wrapped around the top of her head to form a crown. She was a meek person, but had a good sense of humor and an infectious laugh.

"Frieda, show your brother and grandfather your locket!"

"Alright, Papa! I will!" Frieda said as she walked over to Grandfather Brierley.

The whole family attended Frieda's bon voyage party just as they had for Charles, Frieda's older brother, six years earlier when he left for America.

Charles moved to New York in 1905 to marry the widow, Elise Fox. He had known Elise and her family in their small community of Loxstedt, Germany since they were children. Their families had always been friends through the Lutheran church. Charles had decided to ask Elise for her hand in marriage when the pastor had announced to the parish that Elise's husband had died from an accident on the job, and that Elise was in dire need of support, being all alone in America with her two small daughters. Even though she was seven years older than Charles, he felt that he was capable of being the head of the household. He had always admired Elise for her kind and compassionate manner. He sent away his proposal of marriage and was delighted when she replied with an acceptance.

Frieda's parents were deeply saddened to see their oldest child leave home. But at the same time, they were also very proud of his altruism to marry Elise and take care of her daughters.

When Charles left to begin his new life, Frieda was a dreamy 14 year old. She always dreamt of traveling to America. Now that Charles actually lived there, her dream became a goal. She asked her parents when she could visit Charles.

They insisted that she wait at least until she was 20. They really didn't like the idea of their only daughter leaving them for America. Hopefully, she would meet a suitor in Loxstedt and marry before she was 20 and that would be the end of her frivolous dream. But they also knew their daughter. Once Frieda had an idea in her head, there was no persuading her otherwise.

Her mother called her hardheaded. And it was true. Frieda was a determined young woman who always followed her heart regardless of what others cautioned.

"See Grandpapa? It has pictures of Mama and Papa!" she spoke loudly to her partially deaf grandfather.

"Oh yes, my dear, oh yes," Grandpapa William replied in his barely audible voice.

"Look William!" She moved on to her younger brother who was his grandfather's namesake, "Isn't it lovely?" she bragged.

"Yes it is. When do I get to go to America, Mama?" her baby brother moaned.

"When Frieda returns from her visit to New York and you are 21, then you can visit Charles, too," Mama replied. "But now, let's say a toast to Frieda!"

***

Frieda's hope trunk had been packed for weeks. Her trunk had a print of the picture of the Angelus, people praying in the field while the Angelus was ringing.

Most of the passengers on the SS *Friedrich der Grusse* were German. Frieda would have little opportunity to practice her English. Her parents had engaged an English tutor for her before she departed. She was doing very well in speaking English except for her accent. How would she ever disguise her German accent?

Mother always told her to be proud of her German heritage. Catharine was a von Hagen, descending from a long line of aristocratic German landowners. Catharine had inherited the land and the lovely home in which Frieda was born and raised in comfort.

Frieda was confident that America, not Germany, was the land that held her happiness. America seemed to be so much more progressive and modern than Germany. Charles and Elise would often write to her about the excitement of New York. From all of their letters and American magazines that they sent her, Frieda was convinced that America held her destiny!

The day before departure, Frieda, her parents and younger brother, William, took the train from Loxstedt to Bremerhaven so that Frieda would be punctual, knowing her habit of being late. Papa had arranged for the family to stay in a hotel in Bremerhaven, Germany's oldest coastal city, considered the "Rome of the North" during the Middle Ages. The sights and smells of coffee, cacao, tropical fruits, lumber and tobacco filled Frieda's imagination of foreign places as they strolled through the city after dinner. The ship would take the Weser River up to the North Sea then over to England where it would pick up English passengers.

On the morning of departure, Papa hired a horse drawn carriage that brought the family and Frieda's luggage to the dock two hours before departure.

At the dock, the SS *Friedrich der Grusse* stood like a giant ready to take Frieda to America, her promised destiny! Parting from her family was more emotional than she anticipated. Mama cried continuously, and Papa hugged her so hard that she became out of breath. She didn't realize just how much she loved her parents until their goodbyes. Even William cried. Tenderly, she kissed her younger brother on the cheek.

"Take care of Mama and Papa, William." William was only seventeen, but fast maturing into a handsome young man.

"I love you all. Maybe you, too, can visit us in America!" Frieda said in her youthful optimism as tears welled up in her eyes.

"We will see, my darling, God willing," Papa said trying to leave Frieda with a hopeful thought.

She asked them to wait until the ship departed. Frieda was the first passenger to board and check in, so there was no waiting in line. After checking her boarding pass and luggage, she took the elevator to the upper deck where she waved furiously to her parents down below.

"Mama! Papa! William! I'm up here!"

They were patiently waiting for her on the dock below. They looked so small. When they heard her voice, they looked up and waved to her, Mama with her white handkerchief, her face barely showing under the wide rimmed hat with a purple ostrich feather.

"I'll be right back. Don't leave! Stay there!"

Frieda decided to see the second class cabin in which she would be lodging for the next three weeks. She took the elevator down two flights and walked through the narrow corridors until she found her cabin. She plopped on the bed to test its softness, and then began to unpack her small leather luggage bag. It wasn't too bad for a second class cabin.

As the departing horns blew, she took the elevator to the upper level where she could still see her family who were by now sitting in their carriage on the dock. It was much more crowded with passengers. Frieda could see Mama waving her white handkerchief and William waving both arms in a crisscross motion above his head. Papa stood very still. As the ship pulled up the Weser river, they grew smaller and smaller until she could only see water.

"Goodbye Mama. Goodbye Papa and William," Frieda said to herself as she clasped her gold locket and chain. "I love you!"

That was the last time she ever saw her parents and brother.

CHAPTER TWO
Voyage on the High Seas

Frieda stayed below in bed for the first week of the voyage. She was miserable. Charles never mentioned that she might get seasick on board. It took her a week to become accustomed to the rolling Atlantic seas.

On the second week, she was able to join the other passengers. She spent her time playing solitaire, reading books and magazines, and discussing with other passengers their plans in America. Whenever she felt lonely, she would open her locket and gaze at the photos of her parents.

The Captain would amuse the children by having them press his stomach and then emit a large belching sound that threw the children into great laughter. Frieda would laugh sometimes, too.

Finally, the SS *Friedrich der Grusse* arrived at Ellis Island in the early dawn on July 26, 1911. Frieda could not restrain her tears of joy when she saw the Statue of Liberty holding the flame of freedom high above her head, just like the postcard that Charles had sent home. She had finally arrived in America after six years of hoping, saving, praying, and dreaming. This was one of the most fulfilling moments in her life. A large smile stretched from ear to ear that could not be suppressed. She felt euphoric and totally at peace with the world.

Getting off the SS *Friedrich der Grusse* took a long time. After the first class passengers came ashore, Frieda began her walk down the plank where the Captain stood giving his farewells. She restrained her urge to press his stomach as she shook his hand and said goodbye.

She knew that Charles wouldn't be at the dock with Elise and the girls until early evening. Charles knew that it would take some time before Frieda would be processed and released to his custody. He had experienced the same long procedure only six years earlier.

On the ship, most of the passengers were German. This familiarity soon disappeared when she joined with other European immigrants disembarking from the ferries that brought them from their ships to Ellis Island. The unfamiliar sounds, smells, dress, and looks of the people were so interesting to Frieda.

While walking towards the immigration hall, an elderly Jewish man, distinguished by his Yarmulke, faltered in his step and fell into Frieda. She immediately grabbed his arm to prevent him from falling to the ground. His arm was just a bone! He was so frail. When she looked into his eyes, she could see the years of hurt and discrimination that he'd suffered as a Jewish man from Europe. Frieda did not approve of the discrimination shown towards the Jewish people in Germany. It brought her great shame to see her brothers taunting the Jewish kids at school when they were children. She could never understand why some people, even in her own family, could hate, and even worse, harm another group of people.

Once she entered the great hall with all of the other immigrants, she went through a maze of lines where her papers were processed and numerous questions were asked of her; could she read and write English, who was sponsoring her stay in America, what was the condition of her health both mental and physical, and on and on. She laughed to herself that by the end of all of this interrogation, her mental health may be questionable. Frieda's good understanding of the English language enabled her to progress rapidly through the lines. However, some of the immigrants needed translators and were delayed.

It was very sad to see that so many people were retained at the hospital for medical reasons. Some of the families were even split up with young children literally being torn from their mother's breasts and taken away by another relative or acquaintance until the parents were further examined. It was obvious that some people would not be allowed to stay in America.

Frieda wouldn't let these sad situations dampen her joy. She was confident that happiness awaited her. She silently said a prayer for those less fortunate than her, and moved into the large cafeteria where hundreds of people were having breakfast at long wooden tables and benches.

She sat next to a family which included three generations of people: a grandma, grandpa, mama and papa and four small children. The grandma spoke in a language foreign to Frieda and gestured for her to sit down. She offered Frieda some sausage that she had rolled up in a scarf. Frieda graciously accepted, which made the family very happy. The ladies wore scarves on their heads and flower-printed shawls over their shoulders covering their rather plain looking blouses and dark skirts that completely covered their bodies. Their dress was in stark contrast to the fashionable way the models looked in the American magazines that Elise sent to Frieda, but their generosity and warmth made Frieda feel at ease.

Frieda had asked Elise to send her the latest American fashion magazines so that she could be dressed in style when she arrived in America. Frieda and her mother shopped for days before her departure to make sure that she had the latest fashions. Long skirts fitted at the waist with a petticoat and corset, white long sleeved blouses with high collars, and high topped buttoned shoes were the fashion of the day, topped off with a smart straw hat decorated with feathers and flowers.

Her first American breakfast was palatable along with the sausage. Strong coffee like Mama makes, oatmeal with milk and orange juice. She couldn't eat it all because she was too excited.

The cool ocean breeze that blew in through the opened windows gave some relief to everyone from the hot and humid weather. Frieda was glad that she wore her white summer dress, but was looking forward to removing her corset.

Suddenly, the excitement of the arrival caught up with her. She needed to sleep. She had plenty of time to take a nap before Charles and the family would pick her up. She found a wooden bench outside of the cafeteria away from the noise, propped her suitcase and hand bag against the side rail, kissed Mama and Papa's pictures in the locket, and fell into a deep slumber with the distant cacophony of many languages fading in the background. She had arrived! She made it through all the lines of interrogation and examination! Now, she could rest.

CHAPTER THREE
Life in New York

Charles was true to his word and picked up his sister promptly at 5:30 PM. In the six years since she had last seen Charles, he had matured into a distinguished looking young man. After Charles signed the release papers stating that he was her brother and would be responsible for Frieda during her stay in America, they kissed and hugged each other at the "kissing post" where friends and relatives greeted each other. Frieda would be staying with his family at 347 W. 141st Avenue in New York.

While Charles claimed her trunk, she perused the dock area appreciating all the different people and new sights. It was like seeing the whole world in one place! Then she heard someone calling her in German.

"Frieda! Frieda! Over here! We are over here!" It was Elise, her sister-in-law, with her two pretty daughters. They had walked a few paces from their car, a model-T, to greet Frieda.

"We couldn't wait any longer. The girls so wanted to meet their Aunt Frieda! I don't think that Charles would mind. Where is he anyway?"

"Charles went to claim my trunk. I am so glad to see you!" Frieda hugged Elise.

"I am glad to see you, too! Frieda, this is my eldest daughter, Bertha who is twelve and my youngest, Hattie who is nine."

"Hello, Aunt Frieda," said Bertha

"Hello. You are the one who is going to help Mama take care of us!" said the youngest daughter.

"Yes, aren't we going to have fun together?" laughed Frieda as she bent down to hug each of her nieces.

Charles and a porter, the first colored man she ever saw, brought the trunk to the car and placed it in the rumble seat. Everyone boarded and they were off! The ride from the dock area up through lower Manhattan was fascinating. The buildings were taller than the buildings in Bremerhaven and certainly in Loxstedt. There were more people in the streets and on the sidewalks, too! There were more autos than horse drawn buggies. And the ladies were so stylish in their appearance! There was so much to see and experience.

"There are so many people here in New York!" Frieda said to her family.

"I told you that New York would be something that you never experienced back home in Loxstedt!" Charles yelled over the sound of the engine.

***

Elise and Charles had a very well kept but old home in New York. Telling from the interior, at one time it was a fine middle-class home with a mahogany wood staircase and a fireplace with inlaid tile. Charles and Elise had recently installed electricity throughout the home of which Elise was quite proud. They even had a phone in the hallway that rarely rang but was a proud addition to the house at any rate.

Frieda shared a bedroom with her step-nieces on the second floor. She didn't have the luxury of her own bedroom as she had in Germany. However, she enjoyed the company of the girls. They were like younger sisters that she never had.

Bertha and Hattie helped Frieda with her English and she helped them with their German. Sometimes, they would giggle and make fun at Frieda's thick German accent and unique pronunciation of the English language. That made Frieda quite self-conscious and the language lessons would come to an abrupt end.

Her main responsibility was to tend to the girls' needs and help Elise with the laundry. Little did she know that she would greatly depend on this skill for her livelihood later on in life. At home in Germany, there were maids who did the laundry, cooking, and cleaning. But she knew that she would have to make some trade offs in order to stay with her brother in America, so she didn't mind.

Charles worked at a machine factory five days a week, ten hours a day, and a half a day on Saturday. He was a machinist, as was his father, and did fairly well for the family. Elise raised the girls, maintained the household duties, and taught Sunday school at the Lutheran Church. She was the rock of the family.

There was a boarder, Michael Nougolis, who lived in the attic room. Elise took him in after the death of her husband to help with finances. He was rarely at home, paid his rent on time, and when he was home, he kept to himself. So, after Charles married Elise, Charles decided to let him stay. Michael rarely spoke to the family, which was just fine with Frieda.

For fun, the family would take the El from West 144th Street to Central Park where they would leisurely stroll and picnic in a shaded area. It was fun to watch all of the different people taking their leisurely Sunday strolls through the park and listening to so many different languages being spoken by the women in their white organdy dresses and parasols, the men in their white shirts and trousers held up by suspenders and wearing bowler hats.

Occasionally, Frieda would buy an Italian ice from the Italian hurdy-gurdy man for herself and the girls. She thought the Italian men were so handsome with their dark skin, slick dark hair, moustaches, and romantic brown eyes.

It was very hot and humid in New York when Frieda arrived in July. She had never experienced this type of heat in Loxstedt. In the early evening, the family and neighbors would sit on the stoops of their homes and enjoy the cooler evening weather.

To relieve themselves from the stifling heat and humidity, and smell of the horse manure and sewage on the streets, the family would often visit Coney Island. The cool ocean breeze was a welcome relief.

Frieda bought herself a fashionable bathing suit, a frilly little dress that covered all of her body except her lower arms and legs. Of course, Charles complained that it was too revealing. Elise, as always, came to Frieda's defense and put an end to Charles' complaining. The family had fun taking pictures of themselves at the beach with a Kodak camera and sent the pictures to Mama, Papa and William.

Except for these few outings on Sundays, the family stayed at home. This irritated Frieda something awful. She didn't come to America to be shut up in her brother's house! She wanted desperately to meet people her age and explore New York. She did meet one young man, Herman Kruger, at the Lutheran church that the family attended on Sunday. He was polite, but not very interesting. His parents emigrated from Germany and he was born in America. Frieda did not like the fact that Herman was a mama's boy and everything that they did was at the suggestion of his mother. Also, Herman refused to speak German. Elise sensed that Frieda was not interested in Herman for other than a friend.

From this experience with Herman, Frieda learned that the first generation of German Americans preferred and were much more proficient at English than their parents' tongue. Even Bertha and Hattie preferred to speak English, and struggled conversing in German with Charles and Elise.

Frieda surmised that she would have to improve her English in order to improve her chances of meeting a nice American gentleman. For a young girl of twenty, this was one of the most important concerns of her life. So, Frieda practiced English more diligently with her nieces, even though they ridiculed her sometimes. Frieda was certain that being fluent in English would increase her chances of meeting someone!

CHAPTER FOUR
Meeting Bruce Miller

The family celebrated Frieda's 21st birthday on November 6, 1911. Elise invited Herman and some of the young people from the Lutheran church. It was the first birthday that Frieda celebrated without Mama, Papa and William, so it was a bit melancholy. Before she retired that evening, she opened the locket and pretended that Mama and Papa wished her a happy birthday.

Winter came early in 1911. Beginning in early November, coal was delivered on a regular basis by a horse drawn wagon. A chute was attached to the coal wagon which was drawn close to the house where the coal was shoveled through the chute into the opened basement window. The coal then fell into the coal bin in the basement.

While washing some laundry, Frieda heard the horse drawn coal wagon being pulled up by the basement window and didn't think anything of it. Charles had told her that the coal would be delivered that day. Suddenly, she was startled by a loud knock on the back door. Did Elise forget her key to the house? She dried her hands and hurried to answer the door before the person knocked again. When she opened the door, there stood a very handsome young man with black wavy hair creeping out from under a knit cap. He was wearing a black leather apron over a heavy knit sweater. He had a full moustache, bushy dark eyebrows, and dark brown eyes. His face was smudged with coal, but it didn't detract from his good looks. He looked like the handsome Italian men she admired in Central Park.

For a moment that seemed like an eternity, their eyes connected. She felt warm all over especially in her cheeks. She had never felt this strange rapturous feeling before.

"Can you open the basement window, ma'am?" he said in his brash Midwestern accent. "Is your husband home? I've come to deliver your coal, and the window is locked."

"I do not have a brother. I mean I do not have a husband. This is my brother's home. He's not home. I'll unlock the window for you." Frieda was tongue tied.

"Thank you, miss." He was relieved that she wasn't married.

Frieda closed the door and seemed to float down the stairs into the basement where the young man was looking through the window waiting for her arrival. She blushed and felt a bit self-conscious. She reached for the window lock exposing her petite figure and the lovely outline of her breasts. The coal man did not look away or even try to conceal his interest. She felt flattered but also embarrassed.

With the window opened, he asked, "From your accent, you must not be from around here. Where are you from, miss?"

"I am from Deutschland, I mean Germany," Frieda shyly answered, surprised that the words just flew out of her mouth. She usually wasn't this at ease with Americans.

"I'm from Chicago in Illinois. Have you been here long?"

"Since July." Frieda was enjoying the conversation but, the chill from outside was causing her to shiver. The temperature was 40 degrees and not conducive to a long conversation through a basement window.

"My name is Bruce Miller." He reached out his dirty hand to shake hers and then pulled it back, realizing it was too dirty for her to shake. "Sorry miss. What's your name?"

"My name is Frieda Brierley," Frieda said timidly.

"Glad to meet you, miss. Well, I'll start shoveling the coal. I can see that you are cold. Nice to meet you." He smiled showing his perfect white teeth.

"Nice to make your acquaintance, Mr. Bruce Miller." Frieda could feel herself blushing. She ran up the staircase with no effort at all. All of a sudden, she felt a new energy.

The name, Bruce Miller, was running through her mind. Over and over she repeated the scene of their meeting and the words that they exchanged as if watching a nickelodeon at Coney Island. Bruce Miller. What a delightful name!

***

That evening at the dinner table, Frieda felt light and very happy and couldn't eat all of her meal.

"I met a very attractive young man today and he understood my English!" Frieda blurted out unable to contain her excitement.

"Where did you meet such a man who understood what you were saying?" Charles said jokingly, knowing how self-conscious she was about her accent.

"He delivered the coal today. You forgot to unlock the window, Charles, and he had to ask me to open it for him. His name is Bruce Miller," she explained, summoning up his name in her best English.

"Ah-ha, an American! You have found your prince charming after all!" Charles teased Frieda.

"Aunt Frieda has a boyfriend!" taunted Bertha.

"That's enough, Bertha. Well, how delightful Frieda," added Elise who understood matters of the heart better than Charles. "But don't put all your eggs in one basket; you may never see him again. Maybe he was delivering coal just for today. Eat now. You've hardly touched your labskaus that I made especially for you. Here are some pickled cucumbers."

Two weeks had passed and the day had come for the coal to be delivered. Again, Frieda was home alone and couldn't contain her excitement looking out the window every time she heard a noise in the back alley. This time she heard the horses coming down the cobblestone alley. It was a heavenly sound to her ears. So many questions crowded her mind. Would Bruce be on the wagon? Would he remember her? Is it too bold to wave to him through the parted lace curtains of the window?

She peaked out the bedroom window. Bruce was delivering that day. He, too, must have been looking forward to seeing Frieda again because he was looking at every window in the back of the house when he saw Frieda looking down on him.

He waved to her with his whole upper torso. Frieda blushed and shyly returned the wave with her small hand.

"Frieda! Come down! I want to talk to you!" Bruce yelled unabashedly.

He remembered my name! What could he want of me? He doesn't even know me! Frieda ran to the back door, her heart beating wildly. Suddenly, she stopped to regain her composure. Alright. Take a deep breath. Calm down. He must not know that I've been waiting weeks for his arrival. Then she calmly opened the door to her new life.

CHAPTER FIVE
Falling in Love

The first time that Bruce called on Frieda was the first Sunday in December1911. Charles was dumbfounded to meet a colored man and didn't conceal his feelings. Elise was surprised, too, but soon adapted and tried to make Bruce feel comfortable escorting him to a wicker sitting chair in the living room. Bruce was charming and polite. Charles was rude and direct. He didn't waste any time telling Bruce that he didn't approve of his sister seeing a colored man.

Elise could see the potential of a confrontation between Charles and Bruce. She quickly pulled Bruce and Frieda into the hallway and asked that Bruce leave before her husband's rudeness caused any more embarrassment. She apologized profusely to both Bruce and Frieda and then ran into the living room to calm her husband.

There was no changing Charles' mind about Bruce. Soon enough, even Mama and Papa began writing letters to discourage the relationship. So, Bruce and Frieda had to meet secretly, which just added more romance to the courtship, as far as Frieda was concerned.

The courtship with Bruce was a whirlwind of excitement and fun. The issue of Bruce being colored did not change Frieda's amorous feelings for Bruce. She saw Bruce as a gentle and caring soul. Bruce had that American brashness that appealed to her. The world was his for the asking! Bruce didn't have much money, but he took her to fun and exotic places that she had never seen with Charles and the family. The new sights, sounds, and tastes were very exciting! They went to Fulton Fish Market, Chinatown, where she ate Chinese food for the first time, and Little Italy. They rode on the open air bus all over downtown New York, and danced to a popular new song, "Alexander's Ragtime Ball" at a downtown dancehall. Bruce knew all the places to go where the exciting young people socialized. Frieda felt alive!

The first time they became intimate, it was a cold and miserable day in late January. Frieda told Elise that she would stop by the delicatessen to buy the ham for dinner, then meet the children and walk them home from school. She did accomplish all of her errands, but after secretly meeting with Bruce.

Leaving the house, she lifted her skirt out of the snow and walked to the El platform where she boarded the El to 125th Street where she met Bruce. They only had two hours together. Bruce had a surprise for her. He had borrowed a friend's room in a boarding house for the afternoon.

"Here, hold my hand. I have a surprise for you. You are going to love it. Come on," Bruce said while pulling her along the street.

Bruce took her to a neighborhood where there was nothing but colored people. She didn't mind, but some of the colored people looked at her incredulously as if she were invading their territory. She pulled closer to Bruce for security as they climbed the stoop. Bruce opened the front door into what was once a grand home that had been converted into smaller flats. Frieda felt a bit ashamed climbing the squeaky stairs to the upstairs room in the middle of broad daylight.

When they reached the top of the stairs and walked down the dimly lit hallway, Frieda could smell the awful pungent odor of urine and hear muffled voices behind the closed doors. Finally, they came to the last door on the right, and Bruce took out a long key to open the door. The apartment was just one big room with a bed in it big enough for one person, and a discolored and worn wicker chair holding a few pieces of clothing. Whoever Bruce's friend was, he lived very meagerly. Two big windows with frayed and discolored lace curtains looked out on the cold snow filled streets. The room was very cold.

"This is it! We have it for the whole afternoon."

"I can't stay here the whole afternoon. I have to pick up the girls from school and do some errands."

"Relax, sweetheart. You'll get your work done. Now we have a little work to do ourselves." Bruce led Frieda over to the bed and began kissing her and taking off her heavy winter coat.

"Bruce, I'm cold."

"Don't worry sweetheart, we're going to be warm real soon," he said while pulling the covers down on the bed.

"Oh, no, I'm not lying in that bed. It's filthy!"

"Okay, here, come lie down with me." He pulled the covers back over the bed then Bruce and Frieda lay down on top of the covers. Bruce wasted no time in seducing his love, but something stopped him.

"What is this locket that you always wear around your neck? Whose picture is inside? Is it your boyfriend in Germany?" Bruce demanded in an annoyed tone.

Frieda opened the locket and showed him a picture of her mother and father. "It is Mama and Papa."

"Well they don't need to be watching right now." He unclasped the chain around her neck and put it the locket on the wicker chair next to the bed.

"I don't want to lose that, Bruce. It is very precious to me."

The next hour was spent making rapturous love that at first was slightly painful to Frieda, but then quite pleasurable. Bruce was tender and caring.

"Are you alright my love? I'm not hurting you am I?" He looked down on petite Frieda. There was enough room on the bed with Bruce on top of her. They kept both of their heavy winter coats on top of them keeping in the warmth from their young bodies.

Frieda enjoyed the pressure of his body inside of hers and the feel of the honey warm liquid that flowed between their bodies.

"Oh yes, Bruce, oh yes."

The afternoon of lovemaking came to a close when Frieda heard a grandfather's clock in someone's apartment strike 2 o'clock.

"I must go." Frieda got up shivering in the cold and putting on her clothes.

Bruce picked up her locket from the wicker chair.

"Don't forget this, sweetheart. Here, sit down I'll put it on you. I'm sure glad Mama and Papa didn't see that." Bruce put the chain and locket around her neck and clasped the lock then gave her a last big hug from behind.

"I really have to go. I don't want the girls to be waiting for me."

Bruce got dressed, unaffected by the cold, and they walked out of the apartment house and back on to the snow filled streets of Harlem. Frieda felt paranoid that every person who looked at them knew what they had just done.

They would meet like this many times. Charles and Elise never suspected a thing. They thought Bruce was completely out of her life.

***

When Frieda did not get her "monthly sickness" in February and her breasts became tender, she knew that she was expecting Bruce's child. She loved Bruce, but how would he feel about the pregnancy? She didn't want to abort the pregnancy or give the baby up for adoption. No, she would tell Bruce and hope that he wanted to keep the baby, too.

When they met again and she told him the news, he was delighted.

"We're going to have a baby! I'm going to be a papa!" Bruce exclaimed.

"Yes, Bruce. You're going to be a papa."

"Then you'll just have to marry papa."

"Bruce, you are not serious."

"Yes, I am serious. Let's get married. We can go down to City Hall and get married tomorrow."

"Tomorrow? I haven't even told my brother."

"Now, you know Charles isn't going to bless our marriage. Let's just go ahead and get married. We can move to Chicago and live with my mother until I can get another job. Ma won't mind. She's a sweet lady. You'll love her. Besides, she's going to be so happy that I am finally settling down, especially with you, Frieda."

"Please, Bruce. First, let me tell Charles and then we can get married."

"Alright, sweetheart. I'll write Ma today and tell her the good news."

Frieda was happy that Bruce wanted to marry her and take responsibility for his child. Now, she had to build up the courage to confront her brother, Charles.

CHAPTER SIX
Losing One Family and Gaining Another

It took Frieda two weeks to gain the courage to tell Charles that she was expecting Bruce's child. He became so angry that Elise had to run to the kitchen for a glass of water and a wet towel to cool him off.

"You are still seeing Bruce? I thought I talked some sense into your head, fräulein Frieda! Now, you are going to have his child and a colored child at that!" screamed Charles. "Get rid of his bastard child!"

"Charles! How can you be so cruel! Frieda is a grown woman!" Elise cried.

"A grown woman who has been lying to us and sneaking behind our backs! How can you do this to us?"

"I love him and he loves me. He wants to marry me," Frieda said in a barely audible voice, looking down at the floor and avoiding her older brother's eyes.

"Does New York even allow whites to marry coloreds? I hear in some states that it is against the law. What will Mama and Papa say? You know that they don't approve of Bruce. Now that you are going to have his child, they will be heartbroken, just heart-broken." Charles' voice began to crack with emotion and tears welled up in his eyes. He knew that his relationship with his baby sister would never be the same.

"I will leave tomorrow. Bruce has arranged for us to live with his mother in Chicago. Thank you for letting me stay with you, and I'm sorry that I have caused you any trouble." Frieda spoke quietly but firmly. Tears began to roll profusely down her cheeks. She felt very badly that she hurt her family, but she had made her decision to keep the baby and marry Bruce, and prayed that they would eventually understand and accept them.

Frieda left the room with Elise consoling Charles, and climbed up the stairs to her bedroom. The children were fast asleep and weren't awakened by Charles' screaming. Elise seemed to be the only one that understood Frieda's heart.

The next morning, she arose very early, even before Charles. She kissed Hattie and Bertha very softly on their cheeks as to not wake them from their slumber. As quietly as possible, she tiptoed down the stairs to the front door, cloaked in her heavy winter coat and scarf, with one luggage bag in hand. She would send for her trunk when she was settled in Chicago. Before she reached the front door, she heard Elise call from the top of the stairs.

"Frieda, here, take this," she whispered as she scurried down the stairs barefoot in her nightgown, and shawl. "It's some money that I've been saving for a rainy day but, you are going to need it for the baby. Here, take it!"

Elise pressed the small purse into the palm of Frieda's gloved hand, and hugged her. "If you ever need anything, you write to me. I know how hard it is to raise a family." Elise kissed Frieda on her wet cheek and wiped the tears from her cheeks with her shawl. "God be with you!"

"*Danke shien*. Thank you. You are so kind. I love you, Elise."

Frieda had grown close to Elise over the past eight months sharing the household duties and care of the girls. She opened the door and gave Elise one last hug. "Tell Charles that I will send for my trunk as soon as I am settled in Chicago, and that I will always love him." That's all she could say as her throat was choking up with grief. This was one of the saddest times in her life, leaving one family and starting another.

The wind was beginning to blow snow into the house. She turned and carefully walked down the icy stairs holding onto the balustrade. It was a cold and windy February morning in New York. Not many people were on the street, but Bruce was waiting for her at the corner. He saw her walking towards him and ran up to greet her with a warm hug and a kiss.

Elise closed the front door when she saw that they met each other and whispered a prayer for them both.

From that day on, Frieda was excommunicated by her family except for Elise. Elise served as a liaison between Frieda and her family for the rest of her life. Charles allowed their correspondence, but never inquired about his sister and her family. As far as the Brierleys were concerned, Frieda was dead.

CHAPTER SEVEN
A New Beginning with Bruce Miller

Before leaving New York for Chicago, Bruce and Frieda went to the justice of the peace at city hall and were married. Frieda was pleased that New York didn't prohibit colored and white couples from getting married. It was an unceremonious affair, but pleased them both that their love for each other was now legal.

They bought some ham sandwiches and coffee at a small café, then took the rail bus to Grand Central Station where they caught the afternoon train to Chicago.

The train ride was long, arduous, and uncomfortable. They had to sleep in their seats. Being pregnant, Frieda had to constantly get up and use the toilet. However, the scenery was lovely, especially traveling in the countryside. It reminded Frieda of the countryside back home in Germany. Everything was covered with snow, icicles hung from the roofs, and trees were heavily laden with layers of snow that would occasionally fall to the ground. Every once in awhile, a horse drawn sled would dash across the landscape reminding Frieda of childhood rides that she took with her father in Loxstedt.

Once they arrived in Chicago, they were greeted by Bruce's mother, sister, and nephew.

"There they are!" Bruce said waving excitedly to two women and a toddler.

Frieda saw a short, nice looking, middle aged, brown skinned woman with glasses, and a young attractive lady fashionably dressed who was holding a toddler on her hip.

"Hello there. I am so glad to see you. Did you have a nice trip?" the older lady said, extending her arms out to hug them.

"Hi Bruce! Hi Frieda! It's so good to have you back home again! We sure missed you, Bruce!" said the younger lady, reaching out to hug them with one available arm.

"Hi Ma! Hi Sweeze! How you doin' baby boy? Good to see you, too!" Bruce said as he kissed them all. "I want you to meet Frieda!" Bruce put his hands on both of Frieda's shoulders as if showing off a prize trophy.

"Well, I've heard so much about you in Bruce's letters. Welcome to Chicago, my dear!" Ma embraced little Frieda with a warm and sincere hug.

"Hi, Frieda. I'm Virginia, but just call me Sweeze. Everybody does! And this is my baby boy, Raymond. We call him Hinky for short!" Sweeze gave Frieda a kiss on the cheek. "Kiss Auntie Frieda, Hinky!"

"Nice to meet you Mrs. Miller, Sweeze and Hinky," Frieda said in her best English.

"Please call me Ma. We are family now. Well, let's gather your luggage and grab a carriage home. I bet you are hungry. I have a hearty meal waiting for you at home."

Frieda felt a warm reception from the family and immediately took to Ma and Sweeze.

"You know, Frieda, this is the first time Bruce ever road *inside* the train. I guess he never told you about his days riding the rails."

"The rails?" Frieda asked.

"Oh, don't pay her any mind, Frieda." Bruce looked from behind Frieda at his mother and raised his finger to his lips to quiet her from revealing anymore of his reckless youth.

They walked to the front of the station where fresh snow had recently fallen feeling like soft cotton under their feet. Bruce whistled for a taxi that was large enough for the whole family. Before they left, Frieda took a quick trip to the public bathroom to relieve herself one more time. Then off they went to Ma and Sweeze's apartment in Chicago to settle into their new life together.

CHAPTER EIGHT
A Loving Home with the Miller Family

Frieda gave birth to a lovely baby girl on November 1, 1912 at the colored hospital. The local hospital run by whites, refused to service Frieda because she was married to a colored man. The baby was born with no complications and a short labor.

The baby was named Florence Catharine after her grandmothers, Florence Miller and Catharine Brierley. Baby Florence was a beautiful girl with lots of curly, light brown hair, fair skin, and blue eyes like her mother. The whole family just loved this little angel, especially little Hinky, who loved to hold his infant cousin. Frieda only wished that her family could see this precious bundle of joy!

This was one of the most wonderful times in Frieda's life. Even though she and Bruce did not have their own home and had to live with Ma in crowded living quarters, there was plenty of love and goodwill towards each other. Bruce was working in the kitchen of the Palmer House Hotel washing dishes six days a week, ten hours a day. Sweeze was a secretary for a successful colored doctor in Chicago. Ma worked as a restroom attendant in a bank and went out to clients' homes

to wash and style hair. Ma would even wash Frieda's long
blond hair and brush it into a fashionable style.

During the day, Frieda took care of little Hinky, who was
quite precocious, and baby Florence. She was a good baby
and rarely cried except to be fed. Bruce adored his wife and
baby girl. Frieda felt loved, protected, and well taken care.

Charles did send her the trunk, but there was no
correspondence with it. She wrote Mama and Papa to tell
them of the birth of Florence Catherine, but they did not
reply. It deeply saddened Frieda that her family had disowned
her. If only her family could meet Bruce and the Miller family
and see that they were hardworking, good and decent people.
Why did it matter that they were colored? Every time that she
thought about her situation with her family, she would get
upset and start crying.

Whenever Bruce would see her start to cry for no apparent
reason, he knew that she was thinking about her family.

"Come on, sweetheart. They will come around someday.
Don't worry."

"You don't know my family, Bruce. They can be very
stubborn."

By this time, she had stopped wearing the gold locket and
chain that her parents had given her. It was too painful to
look at the pictures of Mama and Papa. She returned the
chain and locket to its box and put it in her trunk. She never
wore the chain and locket again.

CHAPTER NINE
The War to End All Wars, 1914-1918
Frieda's Families are at War

Frieda had made the acquaintance of some Germans who owned a bakery in the neighborhood. It was nice to be able to speak German again and talk about home. However, all the news from home was very disturbing. The *Chicago Tribune* had reported that the Kaiser of Germany had declared war in Europe. Arch Duke Ferdinand of the Austro-Hungarian Empire was assassinated while visiting Serbia. This had inflamed the Kaiser and in April 1914 he declared war on England, France and all the allies to show his might and influence in Europe. Naturally, Germans living in America were deeply concerned about their relatives in the motherland. Frieda felt the same way. Her brother, William, was old enough to fight in the army.

Frieda wrote to Elise, desperate to know about the family. Did William join the army? Are Mama and Papa safe? She even wrote to Mama and Papa, but her letters were returned by the United States Postal Service as non-deliverable. Frieda was mad with worry.

During this time of war, Frieda became pregnant with their second child. Bruce decided that it was time to move into their own home. They found a flat in the Polish section of Evanston about 20 minutes away from Ma and Sweeze's apartment. Ma generously donated some of her furniture to the young family.

On January 16th, 1915, Frieda's water broke and she went into labor sooner than she had anticipated. She woke Bruce in the middle of the cold January night and had him take her to the hospital. The only available transportation at that time of night was the neighbor's sled. Bruce took baby Florence to the neighbor, placed Frieda carefully on the sled making sure that she was warm and comfortable, and pushed the sled to the hospital in the knick of time. Soon after, another beautiful baby girl was born. She had straight brown hair, brown almond shaped eyes, and fair skin showing her American Iroquois Indian heritage from Ma's side of the family. They named her Dorothy Jeanette Miller.

Bruce was delighted with the new member of his family. The first night that Frieda and the baby were home, Bruce left the house to pick up some sandwiches from the local cafe. Frieda began to worry when he didn't return within the hour. In fact, he didn't return until the early hours of the morning the next day. He didn't have any sandwiches for the family either.

"Bruce, where were you? I was so worried about you. Are you alright?" Frieda was sincerely concerned.

"Oh, sweetie, I got sidetracked by some friends and we ended up at the local pool hall."

"The local pool hall? What were you doing at the pool hall?" cried Frieda.

"Sorry about the sandwiches. I'll get some first thing in the morning. I made $25.00 for us tonight playing pool! I'm good at pool." Bruce bragged as he was taking off his clothes and preparing for bed.

"You sleep on the floor. I was worried sick about you, and I am hungry, too! That was very inconsiderate of you," Frieda said indignantly.

Bruce was too tired to argue with Frieda and made a bed for himself on the floor with a pillow and a blanket and immediately fell asleep.

This was the first time that Bruce had ever displayed this type of unreliable behavior. When they were staying with Ma, life was predictable and stable. Was this just a fluke or would this incident become the norm with Bruce? Frieda's mind was racing. Her attention was distracted when Dorothy started crying to be fed. She opened up her nightgown and began nursing her daughter.

Life returned to its predictable but comfortable stage. Bruce was still working at the Palmer House and had been promoted to a waiter. He was bringing more money home from the tips that he made. Frieda was able to buy better quality food and purchase better clothing for the entire family. Life was looking up.

Then, a dramatic change occurred for the entire family. Bruce was drafted into the United States Army. President Woodrow Wilson had declared war on Germany. On April 6, 1917, the United States went to war. Frieda was mortified. Not only was her husband put in harm's way, but her family in Germany was, too! Bruce could be fighting against her brother, William, and attacking the small town of Loxstedt where Mama and Papa lived! Never in her wildest dreams did she think that America would be at war with Germany.

Bruce reported to duty and was placed in the all Negro Army 92nd Division. Bruce's younger brother, Wilson, who was nicknamed Bunk, was also drafted into the same unit. Bunk was shipped overseas and suffered greatly from the effects of mustard gas. Bruce was stationed at home because of a nervous condition. He sent his monthly pay home to Frieda, which provided financial security, but her mental and emotional state was very unstable during the war. She constantly worried about Bruce and William and her parents in Germany. Elise couldn't provide any information because all mail to Germany was discontinued.

When Bruce was on leave for two weeks visiting the family, Frieda noticed a distinct change in his behavior. He began to look strangely at Frieda, cocking his head to one side and holding his hands and fingers in a strange way. Sometimes, he jerked his body parts in order to perform the simplest of tasks. She asked him if he was alright.

"Oh, Frieda, it's just the war that is making me nervous," was Bruce's reply.

Frieda also noticed that he had a voracious appetite for lovemaking. Come to find out, Frieda was pregnant with their third child after his visit home. She informed Ma of the happy event. Ma had been so helpful to Frieda and the family. She would watch after the babies when Frieda did her shopping. Ma was like a second mother to Frieda. Sometimes she felt closer to Bruce's mother than she could remember feeling towards her own.

As the "war to end all wars" progressed, Frieda noticed that some of the neighbors began avoiding her and her German neighbors. One lady had the audacity to call her, a dirty Hun. This deeply upset Frieda. Just because she was German, didn't mean that she supported the Kaiser and his war. There were some Germans who did not support the arrogant Kaiser, and Frieda was one of them.

CHAPTER TEN
The War Ends! 1918

1918 was a glorious year! It brought a close to the war and Bruce's return home! Elise had heard from the family in Germany! Mama, Papa and William were alive and safe!

That year also hosted the birth of their third child, Esther Marianne Miller. Frieda gave Esther her middle name, Marianne. Bruce was delighted with his beautiful daughter as he was with all of his children.

Ma and Sweeze were always present to help at the birth of each child. They were very dear to Frieda, especially Ma, who would take care of the household and the children after the birth of each girl until she recuperated. Bruce liked it, too, when Ma was living with them for that short period. He could spend more time out at night, especially after the birth of Esther. He began to go to the pool hall and hustle pool.

One night, he won a barrel of wine and brought it home with great pride. Ma scolded him for not bringing home some money to pay the bills. When the family was not paying attention, little Dorothy who was three years old turned the spigot on and drank herself to sleep. Ma found her sound asleep by the wine spigot. Frieda was upset with Bruce for not putting the barrel on the shelf away from the children.

A fourth daughter was born on Sept. 25, 1921 in the colored hospital in Chicago. They named her Elsie Virginia. Bruce named her after his oldest sister, Elsie, and his youngest sister, Virginia.

Every time a child was born, Frieda and Bruce would receive a gift and a letter wishing them best wishes from his sister, Elsie. She and her husband, Charles Asa Byrd, whom they called Ace, were traveling from city to city, wherever Ace could get employment as a waiter. For a colored man in the early 1900s, waiting tables was a very prestigious and profitable job. Ace worked at the finest hotels in Washington D.C., New Orleans, and New York. Elsie would also work in the kitchen.

They had just moved to Culver, Indiana where they gained employment at the Culver Military Academy located on Lake Maxinkuckee. They both had secured very good paying jobs. Elsie worked in the kitchen as manager of food service, and Ace as head waiter for the cadets. They were in the process of purchasing a home near the lake. Elsie wrote to Ma and Bruce that this would be a great place to live and raise the children. Bruce could get a job at the academy as a waiter with Ace. Uncle Ace's five sisters and their families were already living there.

Bruce thought that it sounded like an idyllic place to work and raise their young family. However, Ma and Sweeze weren't so enthusiastic about living in such close proximity to Elsie.

"I don't know if living so close to Elsie would be wise. She's not the easiest person in the world to get along with," lamented Ma. "We are used to Elsie's hot temper and outbursts, but Frieda and the children are not."

"Ma, I think living in Culver would be good for the family. If Elsie gets out of hand, I'll handle it. Besides, Frieda gets along well with everybody," Bruce said confidently.

"I'm not worried about Frieda getting along with Elsie. I'm worried about Elsie getting along with Frieda. Well, let's just see. I guess time will tell.

When the baby Elsie was two years old, Ma retired from her jobs. Sweeze had also been forced to retire from her secretary position to the successful colored doctor due to negligence on her part. After the war, Bruce wasn't able to get his job back at the Palmers Hotel, and had to take menial jobs to support the family.

It was time to take Aunt Elsie up on her suggestion and move to Culver. A new beginning in Culver looked promising to all of them. They wrote to Elsie that they would be making the move to Culver at the end of the month.

CHAPTER ELEVEN
Moving to Culver, Indiana 1923

Moving to Culver, Indiana from Chicago was monumental. Packing up both homes and all of the children, Hinky, Florence, Dorothy, Esther, and Elsie, with four adults was quite a feat. Ma packed a big picnic basket of boiled eggs, fried chicken, and apples for everyone to eat on the long train ride from Chicago, Illinois to Plymouth, Indiana. The children were excited on the Nickel Plate Railroad train. The whole family sat in the colored section of the train behind the engine. Frieda followed her husband and sat her and the children down where she was told. She noticed that other passengers had big baskets of food, too. When the train stopped at different stations, the colored people felt reluctant to buy food in the train station restaurants in fear of discrimination. That's why they prepared their own food for the train ride and ate on the train to avoid the whole humiliating experience of being refused. Frieda thought this was one of many inconveniences for colored people to endure.

When they finally arrived in Plymouth, Uncle Ace met them at the train station with two large automobiles, one driven by a fellow waiter from the Culver Academy. The family was covered with soot, and Ma and Frieda were wiping off the children's faces with handkerchiefs when a tall, thin, handsome dark brown man with slick black hair approached them with opened arms and a big wide smile.

"You must be Frieda!" Ace said as he gave her a big hug that almost knocked her off her feet. "So glad to finally meet you." He smiled, tears of joy welling in his eyes. "Ma! How long has it been?" said Ace as he kissed his mother-in-law on the cheek.

"A long time, Ace. Good to see you, dear. Where is Elsie?" Ma asked as she looked around for her first born.

"She is in Culver fixing a great meal for ya'll. She has been cooking since dawn!" Ace exaggerated.

"Sweeze! How are you and Hinky?" He gave her a big hug and kiss. "Look at little Hinky. My, my how he has grown. Elsie is just going to love seeing you!" Ace lifted Hinky above his head and into the air, with Hinky giggling all the way.

"Bruce, by golly. How are you doing, man?" Ace asked, furiously shaking Bruce's hand. "Great to see you. You told us that Frieda was pretty, but not this pretty!" Ace placed both arms around Frieda. "Welcome to our family!" He gave Frieda another hug and a big wet kiss on the cheek.

"Who are all these little ones?" Ace said pretending not to know who the girls were.

"This must be Florence." He pointed to the tallest girl, "and Dorothy, Esther and Elsie! I'm your Uncle Ace!" He then kissed and hugged each girl from the tallest to the shortest.

The girls could sense Uncle Ace's sincerity and promptly replied, "Hi, Uncle Ace."

"Alright, girls. Your Aunt Elsie has a nice dinner waiting for you at home. Are you hungry?" Ace inquired while squatting down to their level with a big infectious smile on his face.

"Yes, Uncle Ace!" the girls screamed in unison.

"Alright, let's load up and go!" Uncle Ace said as he lifted the two smallest girls in his arms. From that moment on, the girls knew that they had a great friend in Uncle Ace.

The autos were packed with people and luggage. Frieda felt comfortable with Uncle Ace who was such a warm hearted person. Surely, Elsie couldn't be too bad with a husband like Ace.

Everyone enjoyed the ride through the countryside. The rows of corn reaching to the sky were ready to be picked. The cows lazily grazed the green fields. Frieda could feel the last days of summer coming to a close. The leaves on the trees were turning gold and crimson.

"Oh, you're going to love it here. I can't wait to take you fishin', girls. Do you like to fish?" Uncle Ace spoke excitedly looking back at the girls who were all fast asleep.

"They never fished in Chicago, Mr. Byrd," answered Frieda.

"Never fished in Chicago? Well, they are going to learn how to fish in Culver. And call me Ace. Yeah, we're going to get along just fine." Ace flashed a reassuring smile.

The sound of the humming engine soon put Frieda to sleep even though Uncle Ace continued conversing. She felt comfortable dozing off with Uncle Ace, and knew he was the type of person who would understand.

CHAPTER TWELVE
Life in Culver

Frieda woke up when she felt the auto come to a stop. She turned around and woke up the children in the back seat. Ace pulled the auto up to a lovely two story house with a beautiful lake in walking distance. The yard was full of bright colored flowers and was very well manicured.

"Here we are!" exclaimed Ace. "We're home!"

Elsie, Bruce's older sister, was standing in the doorway to greet her family. Frieda could see that Elsie was a very good-looking fair skinned lady, dressed in the latest fashion, her hair perfectly coiffed. Frieda felt a bit embarrassed by her own disheveled appearance. Elsie and Ace had done well for themselves, and they had no children so they could spend their money on the fineries of life, which they did.

"Hello, everybody!" Elsie spoke in a very refined and controlled voice.

"Hello, Elsie!" Ace spoke loudly while getting off the wagon. "We made it! Come meet your family."

"Hi, sis!" Bruce yelled.

Bruce, Ace, and Ace's friend unloaded the wagons and

put everything on the screen enclosed porch which was so necessary during the hot summers.

Ma introduced Frieda and the children to Elsie. Elsie shook Frieda's hand. Frieda could feel a cool aloofness from Elsie that she didn't feel from any of the other family members. She noticed that Ace wasn't as ebullient around Elsie, also. Whenever he smiled at Frieda during dinner that night, he would get a cold stare from his wife. Frieda pretended not to notice. That night, while preparing for bed, she asked Bruce if he'd noticed Elsie's behavior at the dinner table.

"Let me tell you, Frieda, Elsie and Ace have gone through a lot. After Elsie had a miscarriage of their one and only baby about five years ago, Ace had a series of affairs. She is just protecting her territory, sugar." Bruce gave Frieda his take on the situation.

"But I am not interested in Ace," said Frieda.

"And he's not interested in you, at least not in a romantic way. Elsie just wants to keep him in tow and let him know who is boss. Just ignore it. Ace will do anything for his family. He's a good man," assured Bruce.

Frieda knew that Ace was a good man. She just didn't like Elsie's suspicious looks and insinuations.

It was good to finally be in Culver. Frieda and Bruce kissed good night and immediately fell asleep on the makeshift bed in the living room. The girls slept on the screened porch with Aunt Sweeze and cousin Hinky. Ma, Aunt Elsie, and Uncle Ace slept upstairs. Soon the house was full with the sound of sleeping people.

CHAPTER THIRTEEN
A Change in Bruce

Soon after their arrival, Bruce, Frieda, and the girls moved into a house that Elsie had found for their family. It was located around the corner from Elsie and Ace, which made it nice for the girls to visit Ma who stayed with Elsie. Sweeze later moved to New York to pursue a career in acting. Ma took care of Raymond.

Bruce's first job was as a waiter at the Academy with Ace. But he just couldn't do the work. He seemed not to be able to concentrate or balance the trays. This was very disappointing to Bruce and especially to Frieda. Making ends meet was always a challenge for the family. Frieda tried to enhance the family income by taking in laundry.

Something was wrong with Bruce. He had definitely changed since that fateful day in 1911 when they met in New York. Now, in 1923, Bruce's movements were jerky, his head was cocked to one side, his speech was slower and often slurred. What was happening to the man that she once knew?

One day during the week, when the adults were at work, the older children were at school, and the younger children were taking naps, Frieda asked Ma over for tea. They settled in the kitchen around the table. Frieda had just made some powdered donuts and tea and offered them to Ma.

"Ma, what is happening to Bruce? Have you noticed the way he acts?"

"Yes. I know, dear. I think that Bruce is getting Bright's disease just like his father. That is what the doctor called it. I'm so sorry Frieda."

"Ma, what are we going to do? Is there a cure for this disease?" Frieda cried.

"My dear Frieda," Ma said as she leaned over and took both of Frieda's hands in hers, "the only thing that we can do is wait and pray. When the time comes, Bruce will have to be committed to the hospital, just like his father."

"There is no cure for Bright's disease?" cried Frieda.

"There is no cure, my dear child," Ma said firmly squeezing Frieda's hands.

Many questions flooded Frieda's mind. What would she do? Bruce's commitment to the hospital was inevitable. It was just a matter of time. How would she and the girls survive? Tears streamed down her cheeks.

"Frieda, when that time comes, I'll be there for you and the children. Don't worry. We will make it through together." Ma tried to reassure Frieda.

Frieda appreciated Ma's concern and love, but she knew that Ma's health wasn't that strong and there was just so much that Ma could do for her family.

"Thank you, Ma. You have always been kind and generous to us. But, you have your own concerns with taking care of Raymond and your high blood pressure. I don't want to add to your worries," Frieda said.

"You and the girls have added so much joy to my life. It is no worry at all, Frieda."

It was getting late. The older girls would be getting home from school soon.

"I better get back to Elsie's. I have to start dinner. Don't worry, my dear."

"Thank you, Ma." Ma and Frieda stood up and hugged each other.

After Ma left, Frieda had to lie down on her bed next to baby Elsie. She gently placed her tired body next to the baby as not to disturb her slumber.

The future looked very dim. Frieda felt confused, angry and hopeless. Why hadn't Ma told her about this disease before? Was there some type of medicine that Bruce could take? How were she and the girls going to survive?

CHAPTER FOURTEEN
Life Turns Sour

Life in Culver could have been idyllic. Life on the lake was good for the children with fresh air, clean and fun sports; skating in the winter and swimming and fishing in the summer. But two things upset this bucolic way of life for Frieda and her family: racism and Bruce's disease. Both of them snuck up insidiously on the family causing great harm and eventual destruction. Frieda felt that she had no control over these two dark areas of her life, and eventually fell prey.

The jealousy Frieda felt from Elsie and Ace's sisters and other colored women in the community made it almost impossible to make friends with any of them. It seemed that Ma and Sweeze were the only women of color who truly loved and accepted Frieda. Frieda wondered why the ladies were so contrary towards her. She loved Bruce and never showed any romantic interest in any man but her husband. The men found Frieda attractive, but they also found her to be genuinely compassionate. Frieda pierced through the superficial and judged a person by his character and heart, not by the color of his skin.

One day while shopping in the local bakery, she overheard the baker and a customer, who both attended the same Lutheran church as she did, refer to her little girls as niggers and Frieda as a nigger lover. At first, she didn't realize that it was her family that they were discussing, but then the baker saw her and abruptly changed the subject. The customer walked briskly by her and out of the store. Frieda turned around in embarrassment and walked out, too.

Was it a sin to have children with Bruce? Her daughters were beautiful, intelligent and well behaved girls. How could they talk about her children like that?

Frieda could see that her beautiful children were treated differently. For one thing, they weren't invited to the birthday parties of their white classmates. There was no socializing at all with the wider community. Even at the lake, the people of color stayed in their area to swim or picnic in the summer and to ice skate in the winter.

The Ku Klux Klan had a very active organization in South Bend, Indiana, which fueled racism to exist even in little towns like Culver. When there were pictures in the *Culver Citizen* of the latest Ku Klux Klan activities that were rampant in Indiana, it would pain and disgust Frieda. Wasn't America a land of freedom and justice for all?

The racism came from both sides. Ma, Sweeze, and Ace were the few people who gave her unconditional love. However, Ma and Sweeze weren't always in Culver. Sweeze had moved to New York to become an actress and Ma would often stay with Sweeze. When the two of them were not in Culver, it was hell for her. To make matters worse, Elsie was a dominant figure and wouldn't hesitate to tell Frieda if she was doing something to her dislike. Even though Bruce promised to "handle" Elsie, he rarely defended Frieda. Frieda being a meek person, would not stand up to Elsie's tirades.

Bruce lost every job that he had while living in Culver. At first, people just thought that he was unreliable. He truly couldn't concentrate and focus on anything. He even was beaten up by stranger that he hustled at the pool hall. Bruce knew that he could always depend upon his skill at pool and make a few bucks, but this time, he lost. He put up such a stink that the person became annoyed and punched him a few times. Bruce wanted to bring home some money to Frieda. When he returned home, Frieda was sympathetic with his wounds, but also furious that he was involved in a fight. He scared the girls who scurried around the house looking for bandages, wash rags, and Mercurochrome to put on their father's wounds.

"Papa, Papa! How did this happen?" cried the oldest girl, Florence.

"Did you fall, Papa?" Dorothy asked as she wiped away the blood from her father's forehead.

"Bruce, how did this happen?" Frieda asked firmly.

"Ah, Papa was just trying to defend his honor, girls." He scooped Esther onto his lap, avoiding Frieda's gaze.

"What's honor, Papa?" little Esther asked looking up at her father.

"In this case, it was $10 in cold cash my angel." He gave her a kiss on the forehead.

The girls and Frieda cleaned up Bruce's wounds and bandaged his right eye and left jaw. After the girls kissed their parents good night and retired for bed, Bruce told his wife the real story.

"I don't want you to play pool for money anymore. I want you to get a real job. I don't want to be the only one who is working for the family," Frieda cried.

"I know, darling. Tomorrow, or when this eye heals up, I'll go ask sis if I can work for her at the clubhouse. I'm sorry, Frieda. I never thought that things would be like this."

Bruce and Frieda embraced and then retired for bed feeling genuine love for each other.

CHAPTER FIFTEEN
Violence Disrupts the Family

In 1924, Frieda and Bruce had their fifth and last child together. Bruce was very happy as always with the birth of his daughter. They named her Frieda Charlotte, giving the child Frieda's first and middle name. She was born at home with a midwife and the care and assistance of Ma. When the baby was due, the other girls were asked to go outside until the baby was born. Ma didn't want them to see all the blood and hear their mother screaming while giving birth.

The labor was long for the birth of this child. Frieda really feared bringing another child into the world when it was hard enough to feed the children she had already. Bruce was unemployed and becoming more and more affected by the disease. He always walked with a limp, tilted his head to one side and flailed his arms. It was very hard for Frieda to watch this disease destroy the man she loved and who was once so vibrant, handsome, and lively.

Frieda was the kind of person who would hold her feelings inside, but one night, she couldn't hold her feelings in any longer. It was late at night, and Frieda had just finished nursing baby Frieda and put her down for the night. The other girls were sleeping upstairs in their beds. Bruce came in from the cold winter night. She couldn't tell if he had been drinking because at this stage of the disease, his crippled condition was often mistaken for drunkenness.

"Hey, sweetie. It is so cold out there. Let me get real warm by hugging you."

"I don't want to hug you, Bruce. I just got all the children to bed and washed the dishes. I'm tired."

"Too tired for a little lovin'?"

"I don't want to make love to you tonight!" Frieda could feel herself getting angry.

Bruce came closer to Frieda and wrapped his cold arms around her upper torso, "Oh come on, sweetheart. How about a little sugar for Papa?"

Just then Frieda saw a butcher knife lying on the drain board. Something snapped in her mind. All the pain and suffering that she had endured from Bruce's disease, the gossip from the jealous colored ladies, the racist remarks from the white neighbors, and Aunt Elsie's mean and cruel treatment of her exploded in her mind and took her over the edge. She impulsively grabbed the knife and swirled around pointing the knife straight at her husband.

"You get away from me! I don't want you close to me ever again."

"Frieda!" Bruce screamed, backing away from her.

"You don't work. You don't help me with the children. I'm sick and tired of it!" Frieda screamed at the top of her lungs, saliva spitting from her mouth.

By this time, the girls were wakened by the commotion and ran downstairs.

"Mama! Papa! What's going on!" screamed the oldest girl Florence.

All of the children were in full view of their mother threatening their father with the knife.

"Dorothy, watch the others. I'm going to get Uncle Ace and Aunt Elsie!" ordered Florence.

Florence ran out barefoot into the cold winter night wearing only her nightgown.

By the time Florence, Uncle Ace, and Aunt Elsie returned, Bruce was sitting at one side of the kitchen table crying with his head in his hands, and Frieda was sitting across from her husband holding baby Frieda, crying and feeling terribly ashamed. The knife had been put back on the draining board. Little Elsie was consoling her father, while Dorothy and Esther were consoling her mother.

"Alright, Frieda. What's going on here?" demanded Aunt Elsie.

"Leave her alone, sis. She wasn't going to hurt me."

"Florence said that she was threatening you with a knife. I would call the police over here and have her arrested if it weren't for the children."

Frieda abruptly got up from the table and ran into her bedroom. The family had never seen this type of behavior from Frieda. Everyone was in a state of shock except Aunt Elsie.

"You girls get to bed now. I'll take care of this."

"I want to stay with Papa," said Elsie.

"I said go!" The girls ran upstairs recognizing Aunt Elsie's tone of voice.

"What happened, Bruce?" asked Ace.

"Ace, please take Elsie home. I can handle it now."

"Are you sure, Bruce?"

"Yeah, I'm sure. It's not her fault. Don't blame her, sis."

"Well, I sure as hell don't see you wielding a knife at her!"

"Please. Just go. We'll be okay." Bruce got up from his chair and gathered his sister and brother-in-law in his arms and guided them to the back door. "Thanks for coming over. We'll be okay. Thanks."

But they weren't okay. That same night, Aunt Elsie called Ma in New York to come home. Ma took the earliest train to return to Culver.

Ma knew that the time had come. Bruce had to be committed to the Veteran's hospital. Frieda, with mixed emotions, agreed.

"Remember the talk that we had a few years ago, Frieda?"

"Yes, Ma. I guess that time has come," Frieda reluctantly conceded.

It wasn't easy to commit Bruce. He wouldn't go voluntarily. He left his home and was arrested for vagrancy in the city park. From there, the police took him in the police car to the hospital as Culver did not have an ambulance service.

In 1925, Bruce Miller was admitted to the Veteran's Hospital where he lingered on with what was diagnosed as Bright's Disease, but later accurately diagnosed as Huntington's Disease. The family visited him frequently at first, but as the disease stole his ability to talk and communicate with his visitors the visits became more infrequent.

In 1934, Bruce Miller succumbed to Huntington's disease alone in the Veteran's Hospital in Marion, Indiana where he was buried with a military funeral.

CHAPTER SIXTEEN
Life without Bruce

After Bruce was committed to the hospital, life for Frieda and the girls was very difficult. To bring in some income, Frieda had to take in laundry in her home. Before she was able to afford an electric clothes washer, doing the laundry was an all day affair. It involved making a fire in the backyard to heat up large pails of water for washing and rinsing. Homemade soap made from lye and lard was used to hand wash the clothes over a scrub board.

In the winter, all of this activity was done inside the home. The pails of water were heated on the big potbelly stove and laundry was hung throughout the kitchen and dining room. During the winter, it was quite inconvenient for the family walking between lines of clothes hung in the kitchen and living room.

Baby Frieda was still nursing, and Elsie, three years old, got into everything. One time, Frieda had to do the laundry in someone's home. She had to take baby Frieda and little Elsie with her. Without her noticing, Elsie pulled down the freshly hung sheets which infuriated her mother. The next time that Frieda had to go out to wash, little Elsie had to stay at home alone until the other children returned from school. Frieda hated to leave little Elsie alone in the house, but she had no other choice. She made it clear to little Elsie that she was not to let anyone in the house or leave the house.

Times were tough. Frieda had to earn all of the money to run the household and pay the monthly bills. The oldest girl, Florence, dropped out of Culver High School to work in Aunt Elsie's restaurant to help her mother. Dorothy, the second oldest, stayed in school, but worked very hard to help her mother in the garden and yard and see after her younger sisters. Esther, the middle daughter, was the artistic child with a beautiful voice and a dreamy outlook on life.

When the girls would ask their mother about her parents and siblings, Frieda would just say that they were dead. This answer failed to satisfy Dorothy. One day when Mama was outside working in the garden, she sneaked into her trunk that was under the bay window in the front bedroom. She opened the trunk and saw the lovely painting of "The Angelus." Then she pulled a jewelry box from the bottom of the trunk. Inside was a gold chain and locket. She tried opening the locket, but it was stuck. She got a small knife from the kitchen and pried open the locket, breaking the lock forever.

To her delight, she found pictures of a lady on one side of the locket and a man on the other side. Who were these people? Just then, she heard the back screen door slam and Mama come into the house. She hurriedly put everything back in its place and pushed the trunk under the bay window. Dorothy never told her mother about the locket, but she always wondered who those people were. Later in her life, Dorothy would find out that they were pictures of her grandparents, Abraham and Catharine Brierley. The locket would also prove to be the key to unlocking other family secrets.

***

After hearing about Bruce and Frieda's unfortunate situation, some of the neighbors, particularly the waiters who worked at the Culver Military Academy, would bring baskets of food to the house that would normally be discarded at the Academy. Every week, Uncle Luther, one of Uncle Ace's brother-in-laws, would bring over food from the Academy that was going to be discarded, such as bacon, sausages, biscuits, fruit and cookies. Frieda was very grateful to Uncle Luther and the other waiters who would give the family food. Sometimes, Uncle Luther's wife would complain about the attention her husband was giving Frieda and the girls, but soon would be put in her place when she was reminded of her Christian duty to serve the poor.

Once in awhile, Frieda received a care package from New York with a card in it from Elise. Elise impressed upon Frieda to have the children baptized in the Lutheran church. However, the girls were now attending the colored Baptist church in Culver. Elise mentioned that Hattie and Bertha were more American than German. They still conversed in German in the home, but only in the home. Charles seemed more melancholy and never mentioned his sister's name. Her brother, William, had married and fathered a son, Hans Brierley. Mama and Papa were thrilled with their new grandson. Frieda thought if only they could see their five granddaughters.

CHAPTER SEVENTEEN
Happiness with Mr. Edward Hilliard

While shopping one day in town, Frieda and the girls passed the local barbershop. The girls were becoming very attractive young ladies and Frieda was still attractive in her own right. When they passed the barbershop, the new barber, a good-looking colored man, was cutting a client's hair. He seemed to be totally engrossed in what he was doing.

After buying a few groceries: a pound of dry white beans, some wieners tied together, a jar of mustard, two large pickles out of a barrel, and a loaf of unsliced white bread, the girls and their mother went home taking the same route. When passing the barbershop again, the barber came outside and introduced himself.

"Hello. I just saw you pass by a few minutes ago, and I want to introduce myself. I am the new barber in town, Ed Hilliard."

"Nice to meet you, Mr. Hilliard. My name is Frieda Miller, and these are my children, Florence, Dorothy, Esther, Elsie and Frieda." Frieda extended her free hand.

"Pleased to make your acquaintance, Mr. Hilliard," said Florence, the oldest girl.

"Nice to meet you, sir," said Dorothy.

"Hello," said Esther.

"Hello, Mr. Hilliard," said Elsie.

"Say hi to Mr. Uh..." Frieda urged baby Frieda whom she was carrying on her hip.

"Hilliard is the name, but call me Ed."

"Yes, Mr. Hilliard, I mean Ed."

"Hi, Mister Healer!" baby Frieda exclaimed.

Frieda was proud of her polite children. "We were just making a trip to the grocery store and getting some fresh air. It certainly is a lovely spring day."

"Yes, it is. Well, enjoy the rest of the day. I just wanted to introduce myself. I cut young ladies' hair, too! Please, come by again. I'm open every day except Sunday!"

"Well, thank you Mr. Hilliard. That is very kind of you. Nice to make your acquaintance. Goodbye. Say goodbye to Mr. Hilliard, girls." Frieda's English had greatly improved since she first moved to America, but her German accent was still very apparent.

"Goodbye, Mr. Hilliard." The girls said in unison.

Weeks passed and Frieda had actually forgotten that she met Ed Hilliard. But he hadn't forgotten. He did some research on Frieda and the girls and found out that Frieda was married, but her husband was confined to the hospital with a terminal illness.

The next time Frieda saw Ed Hilliard, he was at her front door holding a box full of apples and a bouquet of flowers.

"How do you do, Mrs. Miller?"

"I'm fine, Mister—"

"Hilliard is the name, Ed Hilliard. I am the barber. I met you and the girls two weeks ago in front of my barbershop."

"Oh yes. Now I remember. Please excuse me. I've been so busy with the girls and all." Frieda said while drying her hands on a towel.

"Never you mind. Here," he said, handing over the box of apples to Frieda. "Take these apples. They are for you and the girls."

"Oh my, Mr. Hilliard, Ed. What a nice surprise. I'm sure the girls will just love them!"

"I'm sure they will. These flowers are for you! Well, I just wanted to drop these off. Mighty fine to see you. May I call on you and the girls again?"

"Well, well—" Frieda was feeling overwhelmed but grateful. "Of course, Ed. We'd be delighted."

"Well good then. How about this Sunday? I can take you and the girls on a picnic."

"A picnic! How delightful. Well, I don't know what to say!" Frieda replied.

"Don't say a word. I'll call on you at 11:30 Sunday morning, right after church. Don't worry about the food. I'll provide everything!"

"Oh my! Why thank you. We will see you on Sunday."

Frieda closed the front door with her elbow and took the box of apples and bouquet of flowers lying on top into the kitchen. The girls were thrilled when they returned from school.

Mr. Hilliard knew how to get to Frieda's heart, through the girls. He enjoyed it, too. He gave the girls free haircuts, took them on rides in his roadster car with a rumble seat, and took them to such events as the Argus County fair. The girls loved being with Ed, too. They could sense his genuine compassion for them. He was fun! Sometimes Frieda thought that they were taking advantage of his generosity, but Ed assured Frieda that he was having the time of his life!

Frieda also was enjoying Ed's attention. He made her feel pretty again and youthful, a feeling she hadn't felt for years. He bought a phonograph for the family. He would wind up the phonograph and take turns dancing the Charleston and the foxtrot with Frieda and the girls to the new jazz records. There was laughter and fun in the home that had been absent for so long!

"Look, Mama. I'm doing the Charleston!" Esther cried out kicking her legs front and back. "Try it, Mama!"

Frieda tried to imitate her daughters and burst out in laughter.

"Am I doing it right, girls?"

"Yeah, Mama. Isn't it fun!"

There was a feeling of family unity that pleased Frieda to her soul. The girls were pleased to see their mother happy. Soon Frieda and Ed became intimate. It had been so long since Frieda had made love. She felt attractive and desirable. The best feeling was that the girls liked Ed and he liked them, too. They felt like a family!

Ed helped Frieda with the rent and bills. At night he would help the older girls with their homework and tuck the younger girls into bed before reading them a goodnight story. He helped her in the garden, brought groceries and even helped with the housework! He was at Frieda's home so often that it just seemed natural for him to move in, which he did. He packed up his belongings and moved out of Mrs. Jackson's boarding home and into Frieda's home. Then the gossip hit the fan.

Uncle Ace's sisters were appalled. Elsie had to know what Mrs. Jackson had told them.

"Do you know that your so called sister-in-law is having an affair with that Mr. Hilliard? Mrs. Jackson told me that he moved out of her home and into Frieda's home, and with all of the girls, too. Lord knows what he is doing with those girls. He must be having a field day!" said one of Ace's sisters.

"This has gone too far! That little Hun! She's still married to my brother and out there living with Mr. Hilliard! Lord, have mercy. The nerve of her bringing that stranger into the house with all of those girls. I'm going to have Ace speak to Mr. Hilliard! That little Hun, whore!"

Frieda heard the gossip and could feel Elsie's disapproval, but she was following her heart and pursuing that which made her happy. Inside the home, there was happiness and joy that she hadn't felt since first living with Bruce, Ma, and Sweeze in Chicago 15 years before. But, outside the home there were glaring eyes and hushed whispers of disapproval. Even the children were taunted by some of their classmates at school. Elsie and Ace's sisters were relentless. At every opportunity, they were asking him to talk to Ed.

"Leave Frieda and Mr. Hilliard alone. From what I can see, they are happy. Every time I see Mr. Hilliard driving the kids somewhere, they are smiling and laughing. I haven't seen the kids that happy in years! He's not bothering those kids!"

"It's not right, Ace, for Frieda to be living with him! She's still married to my brother!"

"You know that Bruce is never going to leave that hospital. Frieda hasn't been happy for years. I don't see the harm in his living there. They are happy, which is more than I can say for some people," Ace said insinuating about their relationship.

That really infuriated Elsie.

"Ace Byrd! You go over there and get that goddam freeloader out of Frieda's house, now! I don't care how happy they are! The whole town is talking about them. It's not respectable. I want you to talk to Mr. Hilliard and ask him what his intentions are. If he doesn't intend to marry her, I want him gone, do you hear me?"

"Alright, alright." Ace tried to calm down the rage he felt from his wife. "I'll talk to him, but I'm not too keen on the idea."

Ace went over to the barbershop on his next day off. He told Ed that he saw nothing wrong with his relationship with Frieda, but that some people in the community didn't approve of them living together.

"I'm between a rock and a hard place, with my wife and sisters on my back. If it was up to me, man, I'd say nothing to you, but they want me to ask you what your intentions are with Frieda?"

"Well, Ace, I love Frieda and the girls very much, and we have talked about getting married, but Frieda doesn't want to divorce Bruce now, I guess out of respect for him.

She's adamant about that. Maybe she feels that she would be abandoning him, I don't know, but that is how she feels."

"You have asked her to marry you, and she has refused?"

"If the situation was different, I think that she would marry me, Ace."

"Well, some folks say that it looks bad, you living there with the girls and all."

"I wouldn't hurt those girls to save my life. I love those girls and they love me. We are happy together. Believe me. If I could marry Frieda today, I would."

"I believe you, brother, I believe you. I feel badly to have to tell you that if you two don't plan to marry, you are going to have to leave. I'm sorry."

"Okay, okay, I'll talk with Frieda tonight."

That night, he and Frieda did talk and came to the conclusion that he would move out. Frieda did not want to divorce Bruce. She felt that she would be betraying Bruce and the girls might lose any benefits from the government when he died, he being a veteran of the war.

Ed Hilliard moved out of Frieda's home two days after Ace had spoken to him, and moved away from Culver, never to be seen again.

For Frieda and the girls, life returned to its unhappy struggle. Frieda was extremely upset with Elsie. It was none of Elsie's business to interfere with her life. And to think that Elsie and Ace's sisters thought that Ed was messing around with the girls! How dare they! If only Ma and Sweeze were in Culver to help defend her.

Frieda felt trapped in this small town of Culver.

CHAPTER EIGHTEEN
Working for Mrs. O' Callahan

After Ed Hilliard left, Frieda was entirely responsible for all of the bills. Once in a while, Ma and Elsie would help when they were able.

One day, she noticed an ad in the local newspaper, *Culver Citizen News,* for a laundress at the O' Callahan's on faculty row. The Culver Military Academy's faculty and their families lived on faculty row. Mr. O' Callahan was the bandmaster at the Academy. The job was within walking distance and would mean a steady salary and daily lunch.

Ma, who had returned from New York and was now living in Culver, offered to look after baby Frieda and the girls when they returned from school. Frieda applied for the job and was hired immediately.

Mrs. O' Callahan was a very nice person. She became acquainted with Frieda and found out that they both had five girls about the same age. Mrs. O'Callahan offered her children's hand me downs to Frieda. Frieda was grateful!

When Frieda got home and showed the clothes to the girls, they were thrilled!

"Oh, Mama. This is beautiful!" Florence held up a sky blue dress with a belt and lace collar to her body. "I think that it will fit me, too!"

"What did I get?" queried Dorothy.

"Well, let's see." Mama pulled out clothing from the box, feeling excited, too. "Here's a cashmere pullover sweater and a matching pleated skirt that looks like it might fit you, Dorothy."

"Cashmere! Oh, Mama!" Dorothy exclaimed.

"What about me, Mama?" cried Elsie.

"And me, too, Mama," asked Esther.

"Don't worry. Mrs. O' Callahan said there was an outfit or two for everyone!"

"Whoopie! This is just like Christmas. Better than Christmas!" Florence cheered.

Christmas was never a joyous time for the family. Mama could never afford to buy the girls fancy presents or even a *tannenbaum* or Christmas tree. The girls usually went to the Baptist church on Christmas and received token presents from the congregation along with the other poor children of the community.

The clothing from Mrs. O' Callahan was really a treat, except when the girls would wear the clothes to school. Some students would recognize the clothing and tease that they were wearing the hand me downs of the O' Callahan children. Once, even Elsie's first grade teacher, Miss Edna, whispered in Elsie's ear during class that she was trying to look just like Susan O' Callahan. Despite the fact that they were teased and taunted, the girls enjoyed wearing the quality and fashionable clothing, even if it was second hand.

Mrs. O' Callahan was a good employer and a good friend. If Frieda ever had an emergency with the children, she would always understand and allow her the day off. She paid well and offered her a hardy lunch every day. Life for Frieda and the girls was more tolerable working for Mrs. O' Callahan.

Frieda had put the happy memory of Ed Hilliard behind her. She wasn't even thinking of romance or meeting someone. Taking care of the girls and making ends meet was her main concern.

CHAPTER NINETEEN
Meeting Mr. Wolf 1929

Then one day her destiny changed when the laundry sink plugged up.

Frieda walked upstairs to tell Mrs. O' Callahan about the plugged up drain. Mrs. O' Callahan called the Academy and asked for Mr. Wolf to come over and fix the problem. He had done a good job fixing the plumbing at her neighbor's home. He worked as a blacksmith for the Black Horse Troop, the famous horse unit at the Academy, and also did occasional handy work on the side.

Frieda was wringing out the laundry when a tall, thin white man came walking down the stairs to fix the sink.

"Good afternoon. My name is George Wolf. Mrs. O' Callahan told me to come on down and fix the sink. It will just take a moment to unplug the drain and then you can finish your laundry."

"Thank you, Mr. Wolf."

"You can call me George. What is your name?"

"My name is Frieda Miller."

"Nice to make your acquaintance, Miss Miller."

"That's Mrs. Miller."

"Oh, excuse me, Mrs. Miller."

Although their first encounter was stiff and awkward, George, a recent widower, and Frieda developed a friendship which progressed into a romantic relationship. When George picked her up for a date, he never came into the house and never met the children.

Mr. Wolf was a mystery to the girls. They wondered why he didn't want to meet them and take them out like Mr. Hilliard did. They did notice that their mother seemed to be happier when he would drive his model-A in front of the house and honk for her to go with him. She always dressed in her finest outfits, like she did with Ed Hilliard, whenever she dated Mr. Wolf. Sometimes, she wouldn't return until late at night.

Despite Frieda's discreetness, the girls were aware of their mother's romantic interest in Mr. Wolf. The older girls had spoken to Ma about him. Ma became curious and asked Frieda over for lunch one afternoon while Ace and Elsie were at work.

"Frieda, I've asked you over for lunch to ask you about something. The girls say that you have been seeing a Caucasian fellow, Mr. Wolf."

"Yes, Ma. I met him at Mrs. O' Callahan's when he was fixing the plumbing. He's a very nice man and he treats me very well. His wife died recently and he has two grown daughters."

"Well, I'm happy for you, Frieda. If any one deserves to be happy, it's you, dear."

"Thank you, Ma."

"Is it serious with Mr. Wolf?

"Yes, Ma."

"Now, what about your marriage with Bruce? Do you plan to get a divorce if Mr. Wolf asks you to marry him? From what I understand, that was the problem with Mr. Hilliard; you wouldn't divorce Bruce to marry Mr. Hilliard. What about the girls? Is Mr. Wolf going to take five colored girls into his home and raise them? These are things that you have to take into consideration, Frieda."

"I know Ma. I think about these things every day. George and I have discussed these concerns, too. George does want to marry me, but he doesn't want the girls to live with us. He feels that they won't be accepted by his family or the people in his town. He thinks that it will be best if they stay with Bruce's family and continue to be raised in the colored neighborhood."

"What kind of man are you in love with? He wants you to abandon your five daughters?" snapped Ma. She was angry now.

"I don't want the girls to be hurt, Ma. You know how the Ku Klux Klan can be in Indiana. It just might be better for them to stay in the colored community."

"Frieda, they need their mother. Can't you wait until baby Frieda is grown?"

"Ma, that won't be for another twelve or thirteen years. Besides Ma, I'm pregnant with George's baby. The baby is due in April."

"Oh, Good Lord! Good thing I invited you over for lunch today. When were you going to tell us?"

"I was going to tell you at the right time, Ma."

"Then you are getting married?"

"Yes."

"Are you divorcing Bruce?"

"We're looking into it."

"The children? What is going to happen to the children?"

"Ma, I want you to look after them. Please don't let Elsie raise them. I want you or Sweeze to look after them."

"Sweeze can hardly look after herself and Raymond much less her nieces."

"Ma, I'm sorry that it had to come out this way. The pregnancy was a surprise and George is very happy."

"I'm happy for you and I'm angry at the same time. I'm just concerned about our girls."

"I know Ma, so am I, so am I."

"I love you, Frieda, like you are my own child. I just don't know how the girls are going to take this."

They both stood up and embraced each other. Ma hugged Frieda a little tighter and longer. Ma loved Frieda and wanted her to be happy, but the way this all came about angered her, too.

"You take good care of yourself, my dear. I will always love you and be here for you if you need me," said Ma.

"I love you, too Ma."

"Please tell me as soon as possible what you and George plan to do. I want to be there when you tell the girls."

It was hard for each one to let go of their embrace, but they did, and went their separate ways. They had developed a very loving and close relationship since they first met in 1912 almost 18 years before.

CHAPTER TWENTY
Mama Leaves Culver

The day had come. It was in March 1930, the beginning of spring, when Frieda would once again depart from a familiar landscape into the unknown as she had 19 years earlier when she left Germany for America. And again, unbeknownst to her, this would be the last time that she would see her loved ones, this time her five daughters, although, Elsie and her namesake, Frieda would see her again under strange circumstances.

Frieda was beginning to show her pregnancy and the gossip started to spread around town. Elsie now had proof that her sister-in-law was a no good "Hun whore" according to her. And she wasn't going to let her off easy for disgracing her family and her brother. Ma wanted to establish a lasting relationship with Frieda so that she could visit the girls once in a while. She didn't want a nasty departure such as Elsie was creating.

Frieda and Ma had arranged the final day. Mr. Wolf would pick her up at 12 noon Saturday. The three older girls would go see Tom Mix, the famous cowboy, who was performing at the Academy. Frieda kissed all of them except Dorothy, who pushed her mother away. She knew that her mother was leaving and never coming back. She also knew and didn't like the fact that her mother was pregnant with Mr. Wolf's baby. The younger girls, Elsie and Frieda, would stay at home. When Frieda walked out the front door, Ma would walk in the back door. And that is exactly what happened. The little girls could sense that something wasn't right when they saw their mother all dressed up. Her trunk, carrying all of her belongings including the gold locket and chain, was at the front door waiting for Mr. Wolf to take it away. Mama kissed Frieda then Elsie and assured them that Ma was coming and everything would be alright, but the two little girls knew something was not right and began crying.

When Mr. Wolf drove up, he quickly ran into the house only to get Frieda's trunk. Ma was by that time sitting on the couch with baby Frieda on her lap and Elsie at her side, her arms around both of them. Frieda ran over to kiss her two younger girls and Ma again when they heard Mr. Wolf honk his horn.

"You better go, Frieda. We'll be fine. You take good care of yourself."

Tears were streaming down Frieda's cheeks as she once again opened the door and traversed the threshold into the unknown.

CHAPTER TWENTY-ONE
Frieda Loses Legal Custody

Immediately following Frieda's departure, Aunt Elsie filed the legal papers to gain guardianship of the children. This would allow Aunt Elsie assistance from the state to raise her five nieces, and to humiliate Frieda.

Frieda received notice to appear in court in November. She had given birth to a lovely baby girl in April and named her Lela. She looked forward to seeing the girls in court and showing them their baby sister. However, the girls never saw their mother. Aunt Elsie and Ma made sure that the girls were kept at the other end of the courthouse, and Aunt Elsie was the only one to appear before the judge.

Aunt Elsie pleaded with the court that the girls be raised in the colored community with their father's family. She also discredited Frieda as being a good mother.

When it was Frieda's turn to appear before the judge, she asked to have visitation rights to see her daughters. Mr. Wolf had reluctantly agreed to that. However, her plea was denied. The judge felt that the present living situation of the girls was the best choice for them considering the attitude of the public concerning racially mixed marriages.

Frieda collapsed to the chair. The thought of never seeing her daughters again finally penetrated her heart. It was unbearable.

The court awarded Elsie Byrd guardianship of the five Miller girls. Aunt Elsie would receive a monthly stipend from the state of Indiana until each girl had reached the age of 18. Although the stipend went directly to Aunt Elsie, Ma was the one who moved in with the girls and became the surrogate mother.

It was a tremendous adjustment living without their mother who lived only twenty minutes away in the town of Tiosa. However, the girls loved living with Ma. For the next four years, they were a happy family. Ma tried her best to take the place of their mother and provided them with lots of love and understanding.

One thing different was the cooking. Ma didn't know how to prepare sauerkraut and wieners and other German dishes. Their meals were more American style such as fried chicken. The little girls, especially Elsie, hated to see their neighbor slaughter the chicken by wringing its neck until the head fell off.

There were fresh vegetables as there had been with Mama only they were prepared differently. Ma encouraged the girls to take naps in the middle of the day and then change their clothes. Life had changed, but Ma had made it a pleasant change for the girls.

CHAPTER TWENTY-TWO
Uncle Bunk

When Frieda left with Mr. Wolf in 1930, Florence was 17, Dorothy was 14, Esther was 12, Elsie was 8, and Frieda was 5. It was as if the mother hen had left the chicks vulnerable to the big bad wolf. The big, bad wolf in their lives was Uncle Bunk, Bruce's brother. Once Frieda left, he began to visit the home of the girls more frequently. In hindsight, Bunk was also showing the abnormal sexual behavior that is symptomatic of Huntington's disease, to which he succumbed a few years after Bruce. At the time, no one knew he had the disease. The girls were frightened by Uncle Bunk's behavior.

One night, while Ma was staying at Aunt Elsie's home, Aunt Sweeze was visiting, and offered to spend the night with the girls. Ma had high blood pressure, and once in awhile needed a break from watching the girls.

Aunt Sweeze and Dorothy were sleeping downstairs in what used to be Bruce and Frieda's bedroom. Florence, Esther, and Elsie were sleeping upstairs. Little Frieda was staying with Ma at Aunt Elsie and Uncle Ace's home.

Florence had told Sweeze, who treated the girls more like sisters than nieces, that Uncle Bunk was touching the older girls in inappropriate places and making lewd remarks. Florence couldn't tell Ma or Aunt Elsie this fact because they wouldn't believe her and probably would punish her, but she could entrust her secret to Aunt Sweeze. They knew he wouldn't enter the house if Ma was staying there, but if Aunt Sweeze was staying there, there was a good chance that he might come into the house at night.

Aunt Sweeze and Florence thought of a plan for the night. Florence would put a knife in the door frame to keep it shut. There were no locks on the bedroom doors. If Uncle Bunk pushed the door open, she and the others would open the door, push him down screaming at the top of their lungs and run downstairs to Aunt Sweeze's room. Then Dorothy would jump out the first floor bedroom window and get Uncle Ace.

That night Florence stuck the biggest knife that she could find in the door frame so as to prevent Uncle Bunk from entering the room.

"Esther, Elsie, tonight we may have to run out of the bedroom and down to where Aunt Sweeze and Dorothy are sleeping. When I say, run, I want you to run as fast as you can and scream at the top of your lungs. Okay?"

"Why, Florence? Are we playing a game?" nine year old Elsie asked.

"Yes. It's a game. We are trying to get away from Uncle Bunk. You got it Esther?" Florence wanted to make sure that her sisters understood what to do.

"Yes, I've got it," said Esther.

That night, sure as Florence predicted, she heard the heavy walk of Uncle Bunk coming up the stairs. He went straight to the room of the unprotected chicks. He knew Sweeze would be sleeping downstairs. Florence woke little Elsie up, Esther was awake.

"When I say go, run to Aunt Sweeze's room as fast as you can," Florence whispered.

Bunk turned the knob and tried to push the door open. The knife held the door shut for a few seconds. He shook the door until the knife became dislodged and opened it with a jerk. Thinking that the girls were still asleep, he crept up to the bed and put his hand underneath the covers reaching for Florence's legs.

"Go! Run Now!" cried Florence as loud as she could.

The girls pushed the covers from their bodies and screamed at the top of their lungs jumping off the bed onto the floor. Florence gave a big push to Uncle Bunk knocking him on the floor. All of the girls ran downstairs to their parents' old bedroom.

Aunt Sweeze heard the commotion upstairs and got out of bed to open the bedroom door. First Elsie, then Esther and finally Florence ran into the bedroom. Sweeze slammed the door behind them pushing the big chest of drawers in front of the door. She was afraid of her brother, too! Dorothy had since jumped out of the window and ran over to get Uncle Ace.

"You leave us alone, Bunk! Uncle Ace is coming, now!" screamed Aunt Sweeze.

When Uncle Ace arrived, Bunk was gone. Aunt Elsie and Ma arrived soon after. Aunt Sweeze told the whole story to them. Aunt Elsie refused to believe it. Ma was stunned. Uncle Ace was disgusted.

"She's telling the truth, Aunt Elsie." said Florence.

"You remember that's your uncle you're talking about, young lady!"

"Elsie, I believe Florence," Ma defended Florence.

"Why would he break into the house at this hour of the night and sneak up to the girls' bedroom if he didn't have bad intentions, and then run away?" bemoaned Ma.

"Well, I have to hear Bunk's side of the story before I pass any judgment on him," said Aunt Elsie.

"Okay. I'll sleep in the front room tonight. You girls go back to your rooms. Let's get some rest and talk to Bunk tomorrow," Ace instructed.

"Thanks, Uncle Ace. We'd like that," said Florence. The girls and Aunt Sweeze went back to their beds for the night feeling secure that Uncle Ace was sleeping in the front room.

"Everybody okay?" Uncle Ace said loudly.

"Yes, Uncle Ace."

"Yes. Thank you, Uncle Ace."

"Okay. Let's get some rest. Now, don't you worry. Uncle Ace is here."

CHAPTER TWENTY-THREE
Abuse

That talk with Uncle Bunk and Aunt Elsie never occurred. Uncle Bunk stayed away from the family for a few days until the incident was no longer fresh in their minds. When he did return, he only spent time at Elsie's home. He was showing signs of Huntington's disease with the flailing of his arms and, of course, his voracious sexual appetite.

Aunt Elsie either refused to believe Sweeze's story or just didn't want to believe that Uncle Bunk had such evil intentions with his nieces. However, Uncle Bunk was determined to satisfy his sexual appetite.

It was summertime. It was hot and lazy, with a cool breeze blowing off the lake. Ma and the girls were taking the train to Chicago to visit friends. The girls had just finished school and were looking forward to the vacation. The incident with Uncle Bunk had faded in Ma and Elsie's minds. Uncle Bunk had offered to drive the girls and Ma to the train station. He filled the car up with the luggage, but left just enough room for one rider and himself.

"Ma, let me take Esther to the train station. I have just enough room for one passenger."

"Well, how sweet of you, Bunk. That's a good idea because there is hardly enough room in Ace's car."

"Come on little girl, you can ride with me."

Now, Esther was not a little girl. She was 14 years old, mature and a beautiful adolescent. Fearing Uncle Bunk, but afraid to object to riding with him for fear of being slapped in the face by Aunt Elsie, she dutifully got into his car.

"We'll meet you at the train station."

Bunk sped off with his prize in the car, the most beautiful of the five girls.

"Now, we've got plenty of time to meet them at the station. How about having a soda?"

"I think that we better go directly to the station, Uncle Bunk."

"Nah. The train isn't leaving until 11:00 a.m. We've got plenty of time."

Just then, Bunk turned off the road into a wooded area. Esther didn't see any people or cars in this area. He pulled over to the side of the road and shut off the engine.

"Come on. There is a place over there where we can get some soda."

Esther was raised to obey her elders and not question their authority. So, she dutifully got out of the car and followed Uncle Bunk through the bushes. Just when they got out of sight of the road, Uncle Bunk did the unthinkable. He raped his niece.

When it was over, and they arrived at the train station, Esther bolted out of the car and ran into Ma's arms, her dress torn and bloody, her stockings dangling down around her ankles, her hair a mess, tears streaming down her cheeks.

"Ma! Ma! Uncle Bunk did a terrible thing to me. He did Ma. I'm telling the truth. He did!" Esther protested.

Ma didn't want to believe that her son could rape his own niece, but she had no choice but to believe it now. The ugly truth was thrown right in her face.

Holding Esther close to her, Ma turned around with piercing eyes at her son.

"How dare you defile your niece. You are not welcome any longer in Culver. When we return from Chicago, I want you gone! You hear me?"

"Ma, it was only a little fun. She wanted it, too."

"You are a damn liar. That's why her dress is bloody and torn! You unpack that car and then get out of Culver. I don't ever want to see you around these girls again! Ever!"

Uncle Ace and Aunt Elsie said nothing. They were stunned. Ma had never spoken to any of her children like that before.

"Ah, here's your stinkin' luggage. I don't like Culver anyway."

Bunk threw the luggage on the deck. By this time, the other passengers and train porters were all looking at the family and glaring at this despicable man.

The girls had circled around their sister and ushered her onto the train. Ma soon followed. There were no goodbye kisses or waves. Uncle Ace and Aunt Elsie walked to their car silently with their heads down.

That evening, Uncle Bunk asked his sister, Elsie, if he could spend the night. She refused him and requested that he leave immediately. Before leaving, he stopped in the kitchen and grabbed a potato out of a boiling pot. Elsie and Ace couldn't believe how far their brother had degenerated.

Uncle Bunk moved to Washington D.C. and worked at the United States Mint until the disease prevented him from working any longer. There, he was committed to the Veteran's Hospital and died of Huntington's disease in 1940.

CHAPTER TWENTY-FOUR
Living with Aunt Elsie

Although the girls were well behaved and cooperative, the stress of raising a second family at an advanced age began to take a toll on Ma. She suffered from high blood pressure and couldn't take care of the girls any longer. Arrangements were made for the three younger girls to stay with Aunt Elsie. Dorothy would live with the Harrison's, friends of Ma's in Chicago, and complete her high school education. Florence would live with friends of the family in Evanston, Illinois where she worked as a nursemaid. Ma took a much needed rest and visited friends in New York.

For Esther, Elsie and Frieda, living with Aunt Elsie was a living hell. Upon moving in, the girls were instructed to never mention their mother's name around Aunt Elsie. Before they walked to school each day, the girls had to completely clean the house. If it wasn't done to Aunt Elsie's satisfaction, they would be beaten by a hair brush or whatever was nearby. Many times, Aunt Elsie would drag little Elsie by the hair from room to room showing her where she didn't complete her housework. This invariably made the girls late for school.

Many times, the girls were reprimanded by the principal for being tardy.

Uncle Ace could do nothing when Aunt Elsie was on her tirade. He usually left the house, grabbed a bottle of liquor and rowed out to the middle of the lake as far away from Aunt Elsie as he could get.

For all the money that Elsie received from the state for the girls, she didn't lavish it on them. Clothes for the girls were never brand new. Aunt Elsie would makeover hand-me-downs to fit each girl. Christmas was the worst time of year. When other children were receiving toys from Santa Claus, the girls still received token gifts from the local church even though Aunt Elsie received money from the state to afford gifts.

If Elsie was upset with one of the girls, she would yell, "You little Hun!" or "You heifer!" Aunt Elsie rarely gave any praise or showed any affection to the girls. This resulted in low self-esteem and confidence and little self-love. Esther escaped by getting married at the young age of 18 to a bricklayer that she met in New Jersey when she was visiting Aunt Sweeze one summer. Upon high school graduation, Elsie was admitted to the University of Michigan in Ann Arbor, Michigan and moved away the following fall.

With her older sisters gone, Frieda refused to live alone with Aunt Elsie and Uncle Ace, even though Uncle Ace was very kind to her. She begged Ma to be able to live with Aunt Gussie, a friend of Ma's in Culver. Frieda was allowed to spend her senior year at Aunt Gussie's and graduated from Culver High School in June of 1941. Ma, Aunt Gussie and Uncle Ace represented her family at the graduation. Aunt Elsie was not invited.

CHAPTER TWENTY-FIVE
Frieda Meets with Frieda

A couple of months before Frieda graduated from Culver High school, she read in the *Culver Citizen News* that Mr. Wolf had died. The newspaper obituary stated that he had left behind his widow, Marianne Charlotte Wolf and four children, two of them by Frieda and two by a former marriage. The obituary included the address of the funeral home in Tiosa, only 20 miles away from Culver.

Frieda called the telephone operator and got the phone number of the funeral home. She then called the funeral home and obtained her mother's address under the guise of sending flowers to the bereaved widow. She dialed the telephone operator again to get her mother's phone number.

Before dialing her mother's phone number, Frieda held the receiver on her shoulder and said a prayer that her mother would be at home. Then she excitedly dialed the number, impatient for the dial to turn around the numbers on the phone.

"Hello," answered a meek voice.

"Is this Frieda Wolf?" inquired young Frieda.

There was a pause that seemed to be an eternity. "This is Marianne Wolf. I'm afraid you must have…"

"Mama, this is Frieda!" Frieda said excitedly hoping that her mother would not hang up the phone.

"Frieda. I, I, I am surprised to hear your voice. How did you get my phone number?"

"I saw in the *Culver Citizen News* that Mr. Wolf had passed away. I'm sorry, Mama."

"Yes, he passed away last week. How did you get my phone number?"

"I called the funeral home and told them I needed your address so that I could send you flowers. Then I phoned information and got your phone number. I hope that you don't mind, Mama."

"Well, that is very thoughtful of you to send your condolences."

"Uh, yes mama." Frieda said politely getting to the real reason of the phone call. "Mama, I'd really like to see you."

"See me? Today? My children will be home from school soon. I must be home for them."

"I can come to your home while they are in school. I'd love to see you, Mama." Frieda begged crossing her fingers and hoping with all of her heart that her mother would agree to see her.

"Well, alright, just for a little while, but not in my home. How about meeting tomorrow on the morning bus to South Bend? We can have lunch at the five and dime store and return on the afternoon bus before the children return from school."

"You don't want me to come to your home?" Frieda brazenly asked.

"Please understand. It is better that we meet in South Bend where no one knows us. I have to think about my children now. I hope that you understand, Frieda."

"Alright, Mama, alright. I can meet you on the bus that goes to South Bend."

"Frieda, there is one more thing. I have to ask you not to call me Mama. Please call me Marianne. That's the name I go by, now."

"Yes Mama, I mean Marianne."

Frieda knew Marianne to be one of her mother's middle names that she gave as the middle name to her sister, Esther.

"I'll be wearing a blue turban on my head and a gray overcoat. I wear glasses now. How will I know you, Frieda?"

"You will know me Marianne. I'll be sitting in the back of the bus in my blue overcoat." Frieda said with a lump in her throat on the verge of crying, feeling hurt by her mother's conditions of the visit.

Frieda hung up the phone and burst into tears. She almost felt like calling the whole visit off, but she knew that this might be the only opportunity to see her mother. She had to accept her mother's conditions.

Both Frieda and Marianne hardly slept that night. Frieda was anxious to see her mother whom she hadn't seen in twelve years. Marianne was anxious that someone might recognize her tomorrow.

In the morning, Frieda pretended to go to school, but instead, took a taxi to the bus station in Rochester where she could catch the bus to South Bend. She purchased her ticket and boarded the mostly empty bus to South Bend. The bus arrived in Tiosa in less than a half an hour. That was how close Mama lived from them all these years.

There she was standing at the bus stop; Frieda recognized her mother immediately, a short, middle-aged woman with glasses, a blue turban on her head, wearing a gray overcoat and carrying a small black purse. She seemed a lot smaller to Frieda now.

Marianne boarded the bus and moved towards the back. Frieda's heart was beating rapidly with excitement. Surely her mother would recognize Frieda with her big brown eyes and curly brown hair that she used to brush and braid every day.

Just then, Marianne made eye contact with Frieda.

"You must be Frieda," sitting down next to her and shaking her hand.

"Yes, and you must be Marianne," tears rolling down her cheeks.

"Now we mustn't cry." Marianne said wiping away tears from her own eyes with a lace handkerchief, then giving it to Frieda to do the same. "We'll be in South Bend shortly, and then we can talk over lunch. It is my treat. My, how you've grown up to be a beautiful young lady."

The forty-five minute bus ride to South Bend was strained. Marianne kept the conversation focused on small talk until they arrived in the big city of South Bend where they would be anonymous.

When they arrived in South Bend, they walked to the local five and dime and sat down for lunch. Marianne still had the German accent that Frieda remembered as a child.

"Are you still living with Ma?" Marianne asked as they sat down at the lunch counter.

"No. Ma lives in New Jersey with Aunt Sweeze. I live with Aunt Gussie, a friend of Ma's. I refused to live with Aunt Elsie and Ma supported me, too. She made the arrangements for me to live with Aunt Gussie.

"Well good for you! I know that Elsie is a difficult person to live with. What about the other girls?"

"Dorothy attended Howard University, one of the best colored universities in the United States. She married a successful businessman and they have a lovely home in Montclair, New Jersey. She is expecting a baby in October. Elsie attends the University of Michigan and is doing quite well. She was always the brains in the family. Both Florence and Esther are married and live in New Jersey. Florence married a very bright man, a chemist. Esther married a bricklayer. I brought pictures of every body." Pulling out an album of family pictures from her large purse.

"My, how everyone has grown up to be so successful." Marianne said as she leafed through the album. "Bruce, there is a picture of Bruce. How is your father?"

"I am sorry to say that he passed away several years ago."

Marianne gazed away from the album thinking of happier times with Bruce and the family. "I'm sorry that he suffered for so long."

"This is a picture of Florence's daughter!" Frieda turned the page and pointed to a little girl taking her first steps with white curly hair in the black and white photo.

Marianne thought to herself that this was her first grandchild and that she looked astonishingly like herself when she was a toddler in Germany years ago.

"What a cute little girl. What is her name?"

"Florence named her Patricia."

"Well, that is a beautiful name for a beautiful little girl."

"This is a picture of Esther's child, Emory Jr. Isn't he cute? She's expecting another child, soon."

"Oh that's nice."

"Do you have pictures of your children, Marianne?"

"No, I don't carry any pictures of my children. The pictures are on the mantle at home."

"What are their names?"

"Frieda, I'd rather not tell you their names. They don't know anything about my life in Culver with Bruce and you girls. Mr. Wolf and I decided not to tell them about my past. We wanted them to be protected and not be hurt in any way. If people found out that their mother was married to a colored man and they had sisters who were part colored, they might want to hurt them. You know how hateful people can be. I hope that you understand."

"Yes. I understand."

Frieda closed the family album that just a few minutes before was bringing fond memories back to her mother's heart. The waitress served them their lunch.

"Let's take some pictures in the photo booth over there." Frieda said finishing up her hot dog and noticing a photo booth in the store.

"Oh, I don't look—" protested Marianne.

"You look beautiful to me, Mama, I mean Marianne!"

The brief meeting was highlighted with the photo session in the small booth at the five and dime. They boarded the bus and spoke small talk until Marianne got off at her stop. Frieda surprised Marianne by kissing her on the cheek and giving her a tight hug. She had a feeling that this was their last goodbye and that she would never see her mother again. She was right.

When Marianne got off the bus, she turned around and waved until the bus was out of sight. She knew, too, that it would be the last time that she would see her youngest daughter with Bruce Miller, her namesake, Frieda Charlotte Miller.

As Frieda saw her mother fade in the sunlight, she silently asked, "What about us, Mama? Aren't we your children, too?"

CHAPTER TWENTY-SIX
Elsie Meets with Mama

In 1955, Elsie and her husband, Les, were attending his annual Tuskegee Airmen International Reunion in Chicago. They drove from Chicago, Illinois up to Culver, Indiana to visit Aunt Elsie for a few days. Despite the difficulty, Elsie had living with her Aunt Elsie those five years during her youth, she felt an allegiance to Aunt Elsie and visited her almost every summer until her death at 105 years old in 1993. Ever since her baby sister, Frieda, visited Mama fourteen years ago, Elsie had a desire to visit her mother, too. Now, was the opportune time.

One afternoon, Les and Elsie decided to take the trip to Tiosa to see mama. Aunt Elsie still forbade the mention of Frieda's name in her home. So, Elsie lied to Aunt Elsie and told her that they were taking Guy Pearson, an Air Force buddy, who drove up with them from Chicago, sightseeing around Lake Maxinkuckee.

They drove to Rochester and were able to find her mother's home by visiting the fire station and having a fireman point out the house in the plat book. It didn't take very long for Elsie's husband, Les, to find Mama's home in the little village of Tiosa near Rochester. Because they knew that Indiana was a very prejudiced place especially during the days prior to the civil rights movement, Les and Guy ducked down in the seats while Elsie visited her mother. It was a rainy and cold evening and few people were on the streets. That was good because Elsie did not want to cause any problem for her mother or her husband and friend, Guy.

Elsie knocked on the door. In a few moments, a small elderly woman opened the door. She appeared to have been taking a nap. Her dog was barking.

"Hello Mama. I'm sorry that I didn't call first. I am Elsie."

"Wait a minute. I have to get my glasses." said Frieda.

When she returned to the door with her glasses on she said, "Hush Queenie!" Frieda tried to quiet the barking dog. "Let me see. Why you are Elsie! Do come in! Please sit down."

"Hello, Mama. It is so good to see you! We are visiting Aunt Elsie for a few days in Culver, and I have wanted to see you for such a long time."

"How is Aunt Elsie, is she as mean as ever?"

Elsie laughed nervously, "Well, she has gotten nicer in her old age."

"How are the other girls and their families?"

"I'm sorry to tell you that Florence, Frieda and Esther have Huntington's chorea."

"Oh, I'm so sorry to hear about your sisters. I often wondered if the disease would affect them, too. So, you and Dorothy are the only ones who weren't affected by that awful disease?"

"Yes. We were very fortunate."

"It can destroy a family."

Feeling that this was an opportune time to speak frankly about the family, Elsie asked her mother, "Why did you leave our family, Mama?"

"You wouldn't understand."

"But, Mama, I am a grown woman with a family of my own."

Elsie's mother said no more about the subject and just looked away pensively. Feeling an uncomfortable silence in the room, Elsie got up to leave.

"Please, sit down. Don't go. Please, let me show you my home and pictures of my children."

Elsie feigned enthusiasm and interest in Mama's "other" family that she felt had stolen her mother away. She wished her mother was as proud of her as she was of her other family.

Mama showed Elsie around her modest but neat home. Mama didn't have many modern conveniences. She still had an old fashioned pot belly stove in the kitchen like the one Elsie remembered having when she was a child. Mama showed her pictures of her grown son and daughter.

"This is Lela when she graduated from high school and my son Ray in the army."

"Mama, that is very nice, but I shouldn't keep Les and his friend waiting any longer in the car. Would you like to meet my husband?"

"Oh no."

"Well, may I write to you, Mama?" feeling insulted that she didn't want to meet her husband, Les.

"You may, but please don't call me Mama or mention my relationship to you. Lela and Ray know nothing about my former life with Bruce. I hope that you understand."

By this time, Elsie's hurt turned into anger. She wanted her mother to be glad that she came to visit her. She wanted her mother to meet her husband! She wanted Mama to see her children's pictures!

"I'm so glad that you came by. Say hello to your sisters for me. Shouldn't we kiss or hug?" inquired Frieda.

"Well, nice to see you." Elsie extended her hand and shook her mother's hand. Elsie hurriedly walked back to the car feeling hurt and disappointed with the visit. Her husband and Gus were still lying, out of sight and uncomfortably, on the front and back seats.

"How did it go?" inquired Les as he sat up in the car.

"Let's get out of here," tears were streaming down her cheeks.

"That good, huh."

They pulled away from the house and drove down the dirt road. Elsie never looked back. Mama was a different person.

CHAPTER TWENTY-SEVEN
Frieda's Children are United

If Elsie had known that she would never see her mother again, she might have forgiven her, and hugged and kissed her goodbye that rainy night in 1955. Frieda's life came to an end nine years later in 1964 from cancer of the bladder. Even though Frieda was experiencing immense pain, she never allowed herself to have surgery and be put under anesthesia. Perhaps she was fearful of revealing her secret past life while under anesthesia. At any rate, in her later years, she endured great physical suffering by choice.

On Elsie's visit to see her mother in 1955, she saw the photos of her half brother and sister on the mantel. An opportunity to meet her siblings didn't occur for another 30 years.

By 1985, only two of Bruce and Frieda's girls were alive, Dorothy and Elsie. Florence, Esther, and Frieda had all perished from Huntington's disease.

After Frieda and Elsie had visited their mother, Dorothy developed a keen interest in visiting her mother and meeting her half sister, Lela and half brother, Ray, too. While visiting Aunt Elsie in Culver in 1985, Dorothy took a taxi to Tiosa and went into the local grocery store. It was a small town store with a potbelly stove in the center and a friendly proprietor.

"Can you tell me where Mrs. Wolf lives?"

"Mrs. Wolf is dead ma'am. She died in '64. But her daughter lives right up the way. You can see her house from here."

"Oh, I didn't know. Well, thank you. You say it is right up there?"

"Yes, ma'am. See that white house on the corner up yonder? Well, that's where Lela and her husband, Joe Swan, live."

"Thank you. Lela and Joe Swan. How do you spell Swan?"

"S-w-a-n, ma'am."

Dorothy thought that Mama might have passed away, but it wasn't too late to meet her siblings. She walked the three blocks to the house and got the address, then walked back to the store and got a taxi back to Culver. When she returned to Aunt Elsie's, she went upstairs, saying that she had to take a nap, and began writing her sister Lela immediately. She began by saying that she was an old friend of Lela's mother. The letter said that Lela's mother, Frieda, lived with Dorothy before she married Mr. Wolf. Lela responded cordially by sending her pictures of her mother whom she said went by the name of Marianne, not Frieda. The correspondence continued for several months after she returned from her visit with Aunt Elsie. Dorothy began to feel guilty and felt that it was time to reveal her true identity to her half sister, Lela.

Dear Lela,

I have been writing you all this time under the guise of being your mother's friend. It is true that I was a friend of your mother and that your mother lived with me before she married your father because I am her daughter, Dorothy. Our mother had two families. One family with my father, Bruce Miller and the other family with your father, Mr. Wolf. She went by the name of Frieda, and had five daughters with her first husband, Bruce. Her last daughter is named after her, Frieda Charlotte.

We knew of your family, but you never knew of ours. My sisters, Frieda and Elsie, visited Mama in Tiosa. Mama asked both if them not to reveal their identity to you and your brother. Now, that she is deceased, and we are all adults, I feel that it is alright to reveal our relationship, for after all, you and your brother are our siblings.

If you agree, my only living sister, Elsie, and I would like to make your acquaintance. Hope to hear from you at your earliest convenience. Thank you.

                                Sincerely your sister,
                                Dorothy

Lela wrote back almost immediately:

Dear Dorothy,

Yes, you and your sister may visit. My brother, Ray, and I are looking forward to meeting the both of you. When we would ask our mother about her life before having us, she would always avoid the subject. So, there was a big gap in her life that we knew nothing about. Meeting you and your sister will bring us closure about our mother's past.

Please write and tell us when you plan to visit.

                                Sincerely,
                                Lela

The arrangements were made to meet. On a beautiful Sunday, June 26, 1986, while visiting Aunt Elsie at her rest home in Culver, Dorothy, Elsie and Les rented a car and apprehensively motored to the small town of Tiosa. They drove through tall corn fields and finally came to the house with large farm buildings surrounding it. They were quite nervous. Les decided that he should stay in the car as he did 30 years ago. Elsie and Dorothy forced themselves to travel the short distance from the driveway to the front door, fearful of what kind of reception they might receive. Elsie knocked on the front door. There was no answer.

"Oh, let's go home. They don't want to see us." Elsie said after remembering how her mother reacted to her visit 30 years earlier.

"No. Knock again. Maybe they didn't hear us." Dorothy demanded. "We've come this far, Elsie, I'm not turning back."

Elsie tried again, but no response.

"They don't want to meet their Black sisters," lamented Elsie.

Elsie was about to give up when she felt something cold at the back of her knee. She looked down and there was a big black dog who without warning had come behind them. The big black dog welcomed them and showed them the way to the back of the house. They followed the dog who led them to the back door of the new addition to the house. Again they knocked at the door only to be greeted by a smiling pleasant-looking lady, their sister, Lela. Inside was Ray, his wife, Ellen, and Joe, Lela's husband.

Everyone seemed happy and welcoming and they began the introductions. They were seeing one another for the first time in over fifty years!

Ray said, "Dorothy I saw you walking up to the back door and I could not get over how similar your shape is to mother's and your way of walking!" He seemed already convinced that Dorothy and Elsie were related to him.

Elsie told them that Les was outside waiting for them, and they responded "Tell him to come in, too!"

Right away, Elsie went outside to bring Les back so that he could meet everyone. After the introductions, Lela invited them to sit around the dining room table and enjoy a strawberry dessert that she had prepared for this reunion.

Lela and Ray asked many questions of Elsie and Dorothy; how long did mother stay with her first family? How many children did mother have with her first husband? And how did mother keep all of this a secret? Frieda's children quickly surmised that she was very secretive about her past, probably because of the zeitgeist of that time: the negative attitude of most people towards mixed marriage.

"Whenever I asked mother what she did before marrying dad, she would always avoid the subject. She told us that all her relatives in Germany were dead, and just didn't give us much information." lamented Ray.

Perhaps Frieda avoided sharing the truth with Lela and Ray because their father demanded that they know nothing of her former life. Perhaps she was protecting her children from both families from the hateful acts of the ubiquitous Ku Klux Klan who were very active in Indiana at that time. Perhaps, she just gave up fighting Aunt Elsie for the children and settled with caring for just one family. Perhaps, her heart just grew cold and prejudice. No one will ever know why Frieda changed her name and identity and denounced her first family. It is a mystery to this day.

Frieda's children couldn't unlock the mystery of their mother's behavior, but one point of interest really excited them. That was the locket that their mother had.

The subject of the locket was what really convinced Lela and Ray that Dorothy and Elsie were their siblings.

Dorothy described the locket in minute detail and the trunk in which it was kept. Elsie and Dorothy remembered the trunk sitting beneath the bay window in the bedroom in the front of the house with the picture of the Angelus in it. They remembered rummaging through it and finding the locket with the pictures of a man and a woman who were their grandparents. Dorothy recalled finding the locket and being unable to open it.

"I got a knife and pried it open ruining the lock forever!" said Dorothy.

Lela admitted that she had some of Mama's belongings and that a locket was among the few things that she possessed of her mother.

"I'll go upstairs and bring it down for you to see!" said Lela.

Seeing the locket brought tears to Dorothy and Elsie's eyes for it was the broken locket that Dorothy had pried opened so many years ago. From that experience, they all agreed that they were sisters and brother.

Ray stood up and opened his arms. "I believe you are my sisters!"

The family was united. The two daughters from Frieda's first marriage and the daughter and son from her second marriage were finally brought together. Had this been a deep prayer and desire of Frieda's that had finally come to fruition?

The siblings still maintain a close relationship. However, one of the in-laws of Lela did not appreciate the discovery of her mother's past and the newfound relationship to African-Americans. One of the daughter-in-laws of Lela asked Elsie and Dorothy if they were going to put this story on the Oprah Show!

***

Friederike "Frieda" Marianne Charlotte Brierley Miller Wolf lived fifty-three years in America from 1911 to 1964, and had two lives with two families. One family was aware of the other, but the second family had no clue about their mother's past. It was the locket that was given to Frieda in 1911 by her parents at her bon voyage party with her mother, father, brother and grandfather in Loxstedt, Germany that united Frieda's two families in a joyous event.

Florence Catharine Miller first child of Bruce and Frieda

Dorothy Jeanette Miller second child of Bruce and Frieda

Esther Marianne Miller third child of Bruce and Frieda

Elsie Virginia Miller fourth child of Bruce and Frieda

Frieda Charlotte Miller fifth child of Bruce and Frieda

Florence "Ma" Miller mother of Bruce Miller

Elsie Miller Byrd sister of Bruce Miller

Wilson "Bunk" Miller brother of Bruce Miller

Dorothy, Frieda, Elsie, and Florence Miller

Esther Miller

Afterthought from the author

This is a true story about my grandmother and family. When I was a little girl, I always asked why we couldn't see my maternal grandparents. My mother explained that grandfather had succumbed to Huntington's disease. Thirteen members of my family have died from Huntington's disease, and there is still no cure. They are: Henry Miller, his children Bruce, Wilson "Bunk", and Virginia "Sweeze; Bruce's daughters, Florence, Esther, and Frieda; Virginia "Sweeze's son, Ray "Hinky", Florence's daughter, Patricia, Esther's children, Emory, Cynthia, Cecelia, and Patrick.

Racism was the other disease that disrupted my family. When asking about visiting my grandmother, the answer was always no. I knew that she was alive, but I couldn't understand why we couldn't visit her when we visited Aunt Elsie in Indiana. Didn't grandmother love us?

Despite the two diseases that disrupted my family, I truly believe that love and the desire for truth prevailed and brought the two families of my grandmother together and urged me to write this story.

To make a contribution or to find out further information about Huntington's Disease contact:

Huntington's Disease Society of America
158 West 29th Street
7th Floor, New York
NY 10001-5300
1-800-345-HDSA (4372)
www.hdsa.org

Thank you.
Paula M. Williams

Made in the
USA
Monee, IL